W9-CBL-346

The Sand Child

THE
SAND CHILD

TAHAR BEN JELLOUN

Translated by Alan Sheridan

The Johns Hopkins University Press
Baltimore and London

Copyright © 1985 by Editions de Seuil
English translation copyright © 1987 by Harcourt
Brace Jovanovich, Inc.
All rights reserved
Printed in the United States of America on
acid-free paper

Johns Hopkins Paperbacks edition, 2000
4 6 8 9 7 5 3

The Johns Hopkins University Press
2715 North Charles Street
Baltimore, Maryland 21218-4363
www.press.jhu.edu

Library of Congress Cataloging-in-Publication Data

Ben Jelloun, Tahar, 1944–
[Enfant de sable. English]
The sand child / Tahar Ben Jelloun ; translated by
Alan Sheridan.
p.   cm.
ISBN 0-8018-6440-2 (alk. paper)
I. Sheridan, Alan.   II. Title.

PQ3989.2.J4 E613 2000
843´.914—dc 21
00-021128

A catalog record for this book is available from the
British Library.

Contents

1   *The Man*   *1*

2   *The Thursday Gate*   *7*

3   *The Friday Gate*   *18*

4   *The Saturday Gate*   *27*

5   *Bab El Had*   *33*

6   *The Forgotten Gate*   *45*

7   *The Walled-up Gate*   *52*

8   *The Houseless Woman*   *60*

9   *"Construct a face as one constructs a house"*   *69*

10   *The Storyteller Devoured by His Words*   *80*

11   *The Man with a Woman's Breasts*   *83*

12   *The Woman with the Badly Shaven Beard*   *95*

v

13 *A Night without Escape*   99

14 *Salem*   103

15 *Amar*   112

16 *Fatuma*   127

17 *The Blind Troubadour*   134

18 *The Andalusian Night*   150

19 *The Gate of the Sands*   157

The Sand Child

1

The Man

First, that face, lengthened by a few vertical lines like scars dug long ago by sleepless nights; a badly shaven face, worked by time. On it could be read some deep wound, which a clumsy gesture of the hand or a lingering look from an ill-intentioned eye would be enough to reopen. He avoided light: daylight, lamplight, even the light of the full moon. Light laid him bare, penetrated beneath his skin, revealing his shame and unshed tears. He felt it pass over his body like a flame threatening to burn away his mask, or like a blade slowly tearing away the veil of flesh that maintained the necessary distance between himself and others. Without that protecting distance, he would be thrown naked and defenseless into the hands of those who had constantly pursued him with their curiosity, mistrust, even hatred, because they found it difficult to bear the silence and intelligence of his face. Its overbearing, enigmatic presence.

Noise disturbed him. Since he retired to his upper room

overlooking the terrace, he could no longer bear the outside world. He communicated with it once a day, when he opened the door to Malika, the servant who brought him food, mail, and a bowl of orange blossoms. He was fond of the old woman. She was part of the family. Discreet and gentle, she never asked questions; a certain complicity united them.

The noise. The noise of voices, shrill or dull. The noise of vulgar laughter or monotonous singing from radios. The noise of buckets being knocked over in the yard. The noise of children torturing a blind cat or a three-legged dog lost in some alleyway where animals and simpletons get trapped. The noise of the cries and lamentations of the beggars. The strident noise of the badly recorded call to prayer emitted five times a day from a loudspeaker: no longer a call to prayer, but an incitement to riot. The noise of the city rising and hanging suspended just above his room, until the wind dispersed or dissipated it.

He had developed allergies; his body, permeable and irritated, reacted to the slightest attack, absorbed it, and maintained it in all its intensity. Sleep became impossible. His senses were not dulled, as one might have thought, but had grown particularly acute, unsparingly keen. They had taken over all the room in that body that life had left vacant and destiny diverted.

His sense of smell missed nothing. His nose brought him every scent. He said that he had the nose of a blind man, the hearing of a dead man still warm, and the sight of a prophet. But his life was not the life of a saint.

Since his retreat into the room upstairs, no one dared speak to him. He needed time, perhaps months, to collect himself, put some order into his past, correct the dire image of himself that those around him had created recently, meticulously prepare for death, and sort out the big notebook to which he consigned everything. It was his private journal, containing his secrets—perhaps just one secret—and also the sketch of a story to which he alone held the keys.

A thick, persistent fog gently claimed him, protecting him from the looks of suspicion and the curses that his relations and neighbors exchanged outside their houses. That white layer reassured him, helped him to sleep, and nourished his dreams.

His retreat did not upset his family. They had grown used to seeing him sink into long silences or sudden, unjustifiable fits of rage. Something indefinable was coming between him and the rest of the family. He must have his reasons, of course, but only he could say what they were. He had decided that his world was his own and that it was superior to that of his mother and sisters—very different, in any case. Actually he thought they had no world. They were content to live on the surface of things, without making many demands, in accordance with his authority, his laws, and his wishes. Without really talking among themselves, didn't they suppose that his retreat must have become necessary because he could no longer control his body, his gestures, the innumerable nervous tics that could at any moment disfigure his face? For some time now, his walk had ceased to be that of a dictatorial man, the unchallenged master of the big house, a man who had taken his father's place and regulated the life of the household down to the smallest of details.

His back had become slightly stooped, his shoulders had fallen in disgrace; now narrow and soft, they could no longer lay claim to a loving head or a friend's hand. He felt an incalculable load weighing down the upper part of his back; when he walked, he tried to throw his shoulders back and stand erect. He dragged his feet as if he had to pick up his body.

Yet there had been no reason to expect this sudden deterioration. Insomnia brought frequent, uncontrollable disturbances to his nights. But beyond that, ever since a break, a sort of fracture, had come between himself and his body, his face had aged and his walk had become that of a handicapped person.

His death, he knew, would come neither from a heart attack nor a stroke. Rather, a profound melancholy would put an end, probably in his sleep, to a life that was so unusual, it could not bear to fall, after all its years and ordeals, into the banality of the everyday. His death would be as singular as his life, except that he would have burned away his masks, would be naked, absolutely naked, shroudless, buried straight into the earth, which would eat his limbs until it brought him back to himself. . . .

On the thirtieth day of his retreat, he began to see death invade his room. Sometimes he would hold it at a distance, as if to tell it that it had come a little early and that he still had a few urgent matters to attend to. In the night he gave it the form of an elderly spider that was weary but still vigorous. Imagining it in this way stiffened his sinews. At dawn there was no spider. He was alone, surrounded by rare objects, sitting, rereading the pages that he had written during the night. Sleep came in the course of the morning.

One day he heard that an Egyptian poet had justified keeping a journal with the following argument: "From however far one comes, it is always from oneself. A journal

4

is necessary to say that one has ceased to be." His aim was precisely that: to say that he had ceased to be.

And what had he been?

The question fell after a long, embarrassing silence. The storyteller, sitting on the mat, his legs crossed like a tailor's, took out a great notebook from a briefcase and showed it to his audience.

The secret was there, in those pages, woven out of syllables and images. He entrusted it to me just before he died. He made me swear not to open it until forty days after his death, long enough to allow him to die completely. Forty days of mourning for us and of journeying through the darkness of the earth for him. I opened it on the night of the forty-first day. I was overwhelmed by perfume. I read the first sentence and understood nothing. I read a paragraph and understood nothing. I read the whole of the first page and was illuminated. Tears of astonishment came to my eyes; my heart pounded. I was in possession of a rare book, a book containing a secret, spanning a brief, intense life, written through the night of a long ordeal, hidden under large stones, and protected by the angel of malediction. This book, my friends, can be neither borrowed nor loaned. It cannot be read by innocent minds. The light that comes from it will blind those who are unprepared. I have read this book. I have deciphered it for others. You can gain access to it only by traversing my nights and my body. I am that book; I have paid with my life to read its secret. Having reached the end, after months of sleepless nights, I felt the book become embodied within me, for such is my aim.

Soon, my good people, the day will swing into darkness; I shall find myself alone once more with the book, and you will be left alone with impatience. Rid yourselves of the feverishness I see in your eyes. Be patient. Dig with me the tunnel of questioning and learn to wait not for my sentences—for they are empty—but for the song that will slowly rise from the sea and guide you on the road of the book. Know, too, that the book has seven gates pierced in a wall at least two yards thick and with the height of at least three strong men. As we proceed, I shall give you the keys to open those gates. In truth, you possess the keys yourselves, but you do not know it, and even if you did, you would not know how to turn them, still less under which tombstone you must hide them.

But enough. We had better go before the sky bursts into flame. Come back tomorrow, unless the secret book abandons you.

The men and women rose in silence and, without saying a word, dispersed into the crowd in the square. The storyteller folded the sheepskin and placed his pens and inkwells in a small bag. The notebook he carefully wrapped in a piece of black silk and put into his briefcase. Before he left, a small boy handed him a loaf of black bread and an envelope.

He walked slowly across the square and disappeared in the dusk.

2

The Thursday Gate

Friends of the Good, know that we have met through the secrecy of the Word in a circular street, perhaps upon a ship plying a course unknown to me. This story has something of the night; it is obscure and yet rich in images; it should end with a feeble, gentle light. When we reach dawn, we shall be delivered. We shall have aged by a night, a long, heavy night, a half-century, and a few white pages scattered in the white marble courtyard of our house of memories. Some of you will be tempted to dwell in that new residence, or at least to occupy a small part of it, suited to the dimensions of your bodies. I know that the temptation to forget will be great: oblivion is a spring of pure water that must on no account be approached, however thirsty you may feel. For this story is also a desert. You will have to walk barefoot on the hot sand, walk and keep silent, believing in the oasis that shimmers on the horizon and never ceases to move toward the sky, walk and not turn around, lest you be taken with vertigo. Our steps invent the path as we proceed; behind us they leave no trace, only the void. So we shall always look ahead and trust our feet. They will take us as far as our minds will believe this story.

Now, you know that neither doubt nor irony will have a place in this journey. Once we arrive at the seventh gate, we may truly be people of the Good. Is it an adventure or an ordeal? I would say it is both. Let those who are setting out with me raise their right hands for the pact of fidelity. The others may go off to other stories, other storytellers. I do not tell stories simply to pass the time. My stories come to me, inhabit me, and transform me. I need to get them out of my body in order to make room for new stories. I need you. I make you part of my undertaking. I carry you on my back and on the ship. Each stop will be used for silence and reflection. No prayers, but an immense faith.

Today we take the path to the first gate, the Thursday gate. Why do we begin with that gate, and why is it so called? Thursday is the fifth day of the week, the day of exchange. Some say that it is market day, the day when the mountain people and the peasants of the plains come to the city and set up their stalls at the foot of that gate to sell the week's produce. That may be true, but it is mere coincidence. Never mind.

The gate that you perceive in the distance is majestic. It is magnificent. Its wood was carved by fifty-five crafts-men, and you will see on it over five hundred different motifs. That heavy, beautiful gate is the book's point of entry. The birth of our hero one Thursday morning.

He arrived a few days late. His mother was ready on Monday, but she managed to keep him inside her until

Thursday, for she knew that on that day only male children are born. Let us call him Ahmed. A common name. Ahmed was born on a sunny day. His father claims that the sky was overcast and that Ahmed brought the light to the sky. So be it! He arrived after a long wait.

The father had had no luck. He was convinced that some distant, heavy curse weighed on his life: out of seven births, he had had seven daughters. The house was occupied by ten women—the seven daughters, the mother, Aunt Aysha, and Malika, the old servant woman. The curse was spread over time. The father thought that one daughter would have been enough. Seven was too many; tragic, even. How often he remembered the story of the Arabs before the advent of Islam who buried their daughters alive! Since he could not get rid of them, he treated them not with hate but with indifference. He lived in the house as if he had no progeny. He did everything he could to forget them, to keep them out of sight. For example, he never called them by name. The mother and aunt looked after them. He withdrew into himself and sometimes wept in silence. He said that his face was inhabited by shame, that his body was possessed by an accursed seed, and that he regarded himself as a sterile husband or as a bachelor. He did not remember ever having laid his hand on the face of one of his daughters. Between him and them there was a wall. There was no joy in his life. He could no longer bear the mockery of his two brothers, who arrived at the house at each birth with a caftan and earrings as gifts, smiling contemptuously, as if they had already won a bet, as if it was they who had manipulated the curse. They rejoiced publicly and speculated about the inheritance.

You are not unaware, my friends and accomplices, that

our religion is pitiless for a man who has no heirs. It dispossesses him in favor of his brothers, while the daughters receive only one-third of the inheritance. So the brothers awaited the death of the eldest to divide between them a large part of his fortune. The father did all he could to change his destiny. He consulted physicians, fakirs, charlatans, quacks from every region of the country. He even took his wife to a Marabout tomb and had her stay there for seven days and seven nights on a diet of dry bread and water. She sprinkled herself with she-camel's urine and scattered the ashes of seventeen kinds of incense on the sea. She wore amulets and sacred texts while traveling to Mecca. She swallowed rare herbs imported from India and the Yemen. She drank a salty, bitter liquid prepared by an old witch. She suffered fevers, unbearable attacks of nausea, headaches. Her body aged. Her face became lined. She grew thin and often fainted. Her life was a hell, and her husband, always discontent, his pride wounded, his honor lost, treated her roughly and held her responsible for the misfortune that had befallen them.

One day he struck her, because she had refused to subject herself to a last, desperate ordeal: letting a dead man's hand pass over her naked belly from top to bottom and using it as a spoon to eat couscous. In the end she agreed to undergo this ordeal. I don't have to tell you, my companions, the poor woman fainted and fell with all her weight on the dead man's cold body. They had chosen a poor family, neighbors who had just lost their grandfather, a blind old toothless man. To recompense them, the husband gave them a small sum of money.

The wife was ready to make any sacrifice and was filled with wild hopes each time she became pregnant. But at each birth her joy turned to despair. She, too, began to lose interest in her daughters. She resented their presence, hated herself, and struck her belly to punish herself. The husband copulated with her on certain nights chosen by the witch. All to no avail. Each birth was received, as you can imagine, with cries of anger, tears of powerlessness. Each *aqiqa* was a silent, cold ceremony. Instead of slitting the throat of an ox or at least of a calf, the man bought a thin goat and poured its blood in the direction of Mecca quickly, muttering the name between his teeth so that no one would hear it, then disappeared, not returning to the house for days.

The seven *aqiqa*s were all more or less skimped. But for the eighth he spent months preparing in the minutest detail. He no longer believed in the quacks. The physicians could do nothing about what was written in heaven. The witches exploited him. The fakirs and Marabouts remained silent. It was then, when all the doors were shut, that he made his decision to defy fate.

He had a dream. Everything was in its place in the house. He was lying in bed, and death paid him a visit. With the graceful face of a youth, it leaned over him and kissed him on the forehead. The youth was disturbingly beautiful. His face changed; sometimes it was that of the young man who had just appeared, sometimes that of a young woman, fair and evanescent. He no longer knew who was kissing him, but what he was sure of was that death was bending over him, despite its disguise of youth and life. In the morning he forgot the idea of death and remembered only the image of the youth. He spoke of it to nobody, allowing the idea that was to transform his life and that of his whole family to mature slowly inside him.

What idea? you may ask. Well, if you will allow me, I shall now retire to rest, and tell you tomorrow the brilliant idea that this man, on the edge of despair, had a few weeks before the birth of our hero. Friends and companions of the Good, come tomorrow with bread and dates. The day will be long and we will have to pass through very narrow paths.

As you will have observed, our caravan has made some progress on the route to the first gate. I see that everyone has brought provisions for the journey. Last night I was pursued and persecuted by ghosts. I went out and met in the street no one but drunkards and bandits. They wanted to take all I had, but found nothing on me. At dawn I went home, then slept until noon. That is why I am late. But I see anxiety in your eyes. You do not know where I am leading you. Fear not, I do not know, either. And will that unsatisfied curiosity I read on your faces be answered one day? You have chosen to listen to me, so follow me to the end. . . . The end of what? Circular streets have no end!

His idea was a simple one, but difficult to realize, to maintain in all its strength: the child to be born was to be a male even if it was a girl! That was his decision, his unshakable determination. One evening he summoned his pregnant wife, shut himself up with her in a room on the terrace, and said to her in a firm, solemn voice: "Until now we have done nothing with our lives but wait stupidly, arguing with fate. Our bad luck is not our fault. You are a good woman, a submissive, obedient wife, but after you had your seventh daughter I realized that you

12

carry some infirmity within you: your belly cannot conceive a male child; it is made in such a way that it will produce only females.

"I do not hold this against you. I am a good man. I shall not cast you off and take a second wife. I, too, bitterly resent that inhospitable womb. It will be cured, its habit reversed. I have issued it a challenge: it will give me a boy. My honor will at last be restored; the color will return to my cheeks, that of a man, a father who may die in peace, keeping his rapacious brothers from looting his fortune and leaving you in need. I have been patient with you. We have been all over the country to try to cure you. Even when I was angry, I restrained myself from being violent.

"Of course, you may reproach me with lacking tenderness toward your daughters. They are yours. I have given them my name, but I cannot give them my affection, because I never wanted them. They arrived by mistake, in place of the boy I have yearned for. You will understand why I no longer see them or concern myself with their fate. They have grown up with you. They have no father.

"I have decided that the eighth birth will be marked by a festival, the greatest of ceremonies, a celebration of joy that will last for seven days and seven nights. You will be a mother, a true mother, you will be a princess, for you will have brought to birth a boy. The child you shall bring into the world will be a male, it will be a man, it will be named Ahmed—even if it is a girl! I have arranged everything. Lalla Radhia, the old midwife, will be sent for; she will last only another year or two, and anyway I shall give her enough money so she will keep the secret. I have already talked to her about it, and she said that this idea had occurred to her, too. We soon came to an agreement.

You, of course, will be the well and tomb of this secret. Your happiness, and even your life, will depend on it. The child will be welcomed as a man who will illuminate this sad house with his presence, he will be brought up according to the tradition reserved for males, and of course he will govern and protect you after my death. Ahmed will rule over this household of women when I am gone.

"We shall now seal a pact of secrecy: give me your right hand; let our fingers intertwine, and let us bear these two clasped hands to our mouths, then to our foreheads. Now let us swear fidelity unto death! Let us perform our ablutions. We shall pray and swear our pact on the open Koran."

And so the pact was sealed. The woman had to acquiesce. She obeyed her husband, as usual, but this time felt involved in a common action. At last she had her husband's confidence. Her life would have a meaning.

The great day, the day of the birth arrived. The woman still entertained some hope: perhaps destiny would at last give her true joy and make deceit unnecessary. Alas! Destiny was obstinate.

Lalla Radhia had been at the house since Monday. She prepared for this birth with great care. She knew that it would be exceptional and perhaps the last of her long career. The daughters did not understand why there was so much bustle and excitement. Lalla Radhia whispered to them that the child that was about to be born would be a male. Her intuition had never betrayed her, she said; such things were beyond the powers of reason. She felt, from the way the child moved in its mother's belly, that it could only be a boy. It kicked with a brutality that could only be that of a male! The daughters were perplexed. Such a birth would utterly transform their family. They looked at one another and said not a word. In any case, there was nothing exciting about their lives. Perhaps a brother might come to love them! The rumor was already running through the district and the rest of the family: Hajji Ahmed was to have a boy. . . .

Now, my friends, time is running out. We are no longer spectators; we, too, have embarked on a story that may well bury us all in the same cemetery. For the will of heaven, the will of God, will be set ablaze by lies. A stream will be diverted, will swell and become a river that will flood peaceful homesteads. O my friends! That sudden, dazzling light is suspect—it precedes darkness.

Raise your right hands and say after me: Welcome, O being from afar, face of error, innocence of the lie, double of the shadow, O thou so much awaited, so much desired; thou hast been summoned to outwit destiny; thou bringest joy but not happiness; thou erectest a tent in the desert, but it is the dwelling of the wind; thou art a city of ashes; thy life will be long, a trial by fire and by patience. Welcome! O thou, the day and the sun! Thou wilt hate evil, but who knows whether thou shalt do good. . . . Welcome . . . Welcome!

As I was telling you . . .

The whole family was summoned and gathered in the hajji's household on Wednesday evening. Aunt Aysha ran hither and thither, as if demented. The two brothers arrived with wives and children, worried and impatient. Close and distant cousins were also invited. Lalla Radhia shut herself up with the hajji's wife. Strict orders were given that they should not be disturbed. Black women in the kitchen prepared the dinner.

About midnight moans were heard: the first labor pains. Old women called upon the Prophet Mohammed. The hajji walked up and down in the street. His brothers held a council of war, whispering to one another in a corner of the reception room. The children slept where they had just eaten. The silence of the night was interrupted only by the cries of pain. Lalla Radhia said nothing. She heated the bowls of water and laid out the swaddling clothes. Everyone was asleep except the hajji, the midwife, and the two brothers.

At dawn, the call to prayer was heard. A few shadowy figures rose like sleepwalkers and said their prayers. The wife was now yelling in pain. As day broke over the household, everything was in great disorder. The black cooks now prepared the breakfast soup, the soup of birth and baptism. The brothers had to go off to work. The children considered themselves on vacation and went on playing in the entrance of the house.

About ten o'clock in the morning, the morning of that historic Thursday, while everyone was gathered outside the birth room, Lalla Radhia opened the door a fraction and gave a cry of joy, then repeated breathlessly: "It's a man, a man, a man. . . ." The hajji arrived in the midst of this gathering like a prince. The children kissed his hand. The women welcomed him with frightened stammering interspersed with praise and such prayers as "May God preserve him"; "The sun has risen"; "Darkness is banished"; "God is great"; "God is with you."

He entered the room, locked the door, and told Lalla Radhia to remove the swaddling clothes from the new-born. It was a girl. His wife veiled her face to weep. Holding the baby in his left arm, he pulled his wife's veil away violently and said to her: "Why those tears? I hope you are weeping for joy! Look, look closely, it's a boy! There's no need to hide your face. You must be proud. . . . After fifteen years of marriage you have at last given me a child, a boy. My first child. Look how handsome he is, touch his little testicles, his penis; he's a man!"

Then, turning to the midwife, he told her to take care of the boy and to let no one come near him. He left the room, wearing a broad smile. . . . On his face and shoulders could be seen all the virility of the world! At fifty, he felt as lighthearted as a young man. He had already forgotten— or perhaps pretended to—that he had arranged everything. Though he had certainly seen a daughter, he firmly believed it was a boy.

O my companions, our story is only at its beginning, and already the vertigo of words dries my tongue. My saliva has run out, my bones are tired. We are all victims of our madness, buried as it is in trenches of desire that must not be named. Let us beware of calling up the angel who has two faces and inhabits our fantasies. Face of the immobile sun. Face of the murdering moon. The angel swings from face to face according to the life we dance, on an invisible thread.

My friends, if you do not see me tomorrow, know that the angel has swung to the side of the precipice and death.

3

The Friday Gate

It is some days now since we were woven together by the woolen threads of the same story. The threads go from me to you, from each of you back to me. They are fragile, yet they bind us together as in a pact. But let us leave the first gate, which an invisible hand will shut behind us. The Friday gate is the one that brings people together, for the repose of the body, the recollection of the soul, and the celebration of the day. It opens to reveal family festivities, a clement sky, a fruitful earth, a man who has recovered his honor, and a woman who is recognized at last as a mother. This gate will allow only happiness to pass through it. That is its function, or at least such is its reputation. Each of us has seen that gate open onto his nights, to illuminate them for a brief moment. This gate belongs to no wall. It is the only gate that moves in step with destiny—and it stops only for those who do not care for their destiny. Otherwise what purpose would it serve? It was through this gate that Lalla Radhia entered.

The feast to celebrate the *aqiqa* was of untold splendor. An ox was killed for the naming of the child: he was to be called Mohammed Ahmed, son of Hajji Ahmed. The guests prayed behind the grand fakirs and mufti of the city. Dishes of food were distributed to the poor. That fine day was to live long in people's memories; indeed, even today everyone remembers it. When they speak of that day they remember the strength of the ox, which ran around the courtyard after its head was cut off; the twenty low tables laden with whole sheep; the Andalusian music played by the grand orchestra of Mulay Ahmed Lukili. . . .

The festivities lasted several days. The baby was shown to the guests from afar. No one was allowed to touch him. Only Lalla Radhia and the mother took care of him. The seven daughters were kept at a distance. The father told them that from now on they were to show their brother, Ahmed, the same respect as they showed him. They lowered their eyes and said not a word. Seldom was there a man so ready to communicate and share his joy. He bought a half-page in the great national newspaper and had his photograph printed in it, followed by the following text:

GOD IS MERCIFUL

He has illuminated the life and home of your servant and devoted potter Hajji Ahmed Suleyman. A boy—may God protect him and bring him long life—was born on Thursday at 10:00 A.M. We have called him Mohammed Ahmed. This birth will bring fertility to the land, peace and prosperity to the country. Long live Ahmed! Long live Morocco!

This announcement in the newspaper set tongues wagging: people did not usually display their private life so publicly. Hajji Ahmed cared not a fig. For him the important thing was to bring the news to the knowledge of as many people as possible. The last sentence also caused a stir. The French police did not at all care for the "Long live Morocco!" The nationalist militants did not know that this rich craftsman was also a good patriot.

The political aspect of the announcement was soon forgotten, but the whole town remembered the birth of Ahmed long afterward.

Throughout the year, the household experienced joy, laughter, and festivities. Anything was a pretext to bring in an orchestra, to sing and dance, to celebrate the prince's first stammered word or first few stumbling steps. The ceremony of the barber was to last two days. Ahmed's hair was cut and his eyes were made up with kohl. He was dressed in a white jellaba, a red fez was put on his head, and he was seated on a rocking horse. The mother then took him off to visit the town saint. She carried him on her back and walked seven times around the tomb, praying to the saint to intercede with God that Ahmed might be protected from the evil eye, from sickness, and from the jealousy of the curious. The child bawled among that crowd of women pushing their way forward to touch the black cloak that covered the tomb.

The child grew up amid almost daily euphoria. The father was thinking of the ordeal of circumcision. What was he to do? How could an imaginary foreskin be cut off? Yet how could one avoid celebrating in great splendor the transition of this child to the age of man? O my friends, there are follies unknown even to the devil! How could the father overcome this difficulty and promote his plan? Of course, he could, you might say, have some other child circumcised in place of his son. But this entailed a risk—

the truth would be known sooner or later. No, his son was presented to the barber-circumciser, the legs were spread, and something was cut. Blood flowed, spattering the child's thighs and the barber's face. The child cried, and was laden with presents brought by the whole family. Very few people noticed that the father had a bandage around the index finger of his right hand. He concealed it very well. And no one thought for a second that the blood they had seen came from that finger! Hajji Ahmed was a very determined man.

And who, in that family, felt he had the authority to confront Hajji Ahmed? Not even his two brothers. Whatever their suspicions, they never dared risk a dubious joke or an insinuation on the subject of the child's sex. Everything was proceeding as the father had expected and hoped. Ahmed grew up in accordance with the instructions laid down by his father, who assumed personal responsibility for his upbringing. The festivities over, the child had to be turned into a man. A real man. Each month the barber arrived to cut his hair. Ahmed went with other boys to a private Koranic school. He did not play much, and seldom loitered in the street outside. Like all the children of his age, he accompanied his mother to the Moorish baths.

You know how that place impressed all of us when we were small. We all emerged from it unscathed . . . or so it seemed. For Ahmed it was not a trauma but a strange, bitter discovery. I know this because he speaks of it in his journal. Allow me to open the page and I will read to you what he wrote about those outings into the moist fog:

In a small basket my mother placed oranges, soft-boiled eggs, and red olives marinated in lemon juice. She wore a shawl over her head, which covered the henna she had put in her hair the night before. I did not have henna in my hair. When I wanted her to put some on, she forbade it and said, "Only girls put henna in their hair!" I said nothing and followed her to the hammam.

I knew we would spend the whole afternoon there. I would get bored, but I had no choice. In fact, I would have preferred to go to the baths with my father. He always bathed very quickly and spared me all that interminable ceremonial. For my mother it was an opportunity to get out of the house, to meet other women, and to gossip while washing. Meanwhile, I was dying of boredom. I had cramps in my stomach and was nearly stifled by the thick, wet vapor that enveloped me.

My mother forgot all about me. She set up her buckets of hot water and talked to her neighbors. They all spoke at the same time. It didn't matter what they said—they just went on talking. They behaved as if they were in a salon where it was indispensable for their health to talk. Words and sentences flowed on every side, and since the room was dark and enclosed, they seemed to be suspended in the steam above the women's heads. I saw some words slowly rise and hit the damp ceiling. There they melted in contact with the stone and fell back on my face as drops of water. It amused me. The ceiling was like a writing table. Not everything that was written on it was intelligible. But since I had to pass the time somehow, I puzzled through those lines. A few words fell more often and more quickly than others, like, for example, "night," "back," "breasts," "thumb"—scarcely had they been spoken when they dripped in my face. I brushed them aside, until other words and other images fell. Curiously, the drops that fell on me were salty. I told myself that the words had the savor of life. For all those women, life was limited. It did not amount to much more than cooking, housework, waiting around, and, once a week, a restful afternoon in the hammam. I was secretly pleased that I did not belong to that limited world.

I juggled with the words and sometimes made pseudosentences fall on my head, such as "At night the sun on my back in a corridor where the man's thumb my man in the gate of heaven laughter . . ." Then, suddenly, a sentence that made sense would fall: "The water is hot" or "Give me some of your cold water." These sentences did not have time to be raised to the ceiling by the steam. They were spoken in an ordinary, offhand way—they were not part of the gossip. I paid no attention to them, empty sentences incapable of stirring my imagination.

Some words fascinated me because they were spoken seldom and softly—words like *"mani," "qlaui,"* or *"tabun."* I later learned that these pertained to sex and that the women did not have the right to use them. Such words did not fall. They stuck to the stone ceiling, which they impregnated with all their dirty whitish or brown imprint. Once there was an argument between two women over a bucket and they exchanged insults. These words kept recurring, shouted, and I took great pleasure collecting them secretly, like rain, in my underpants! I was embarrassed and sometimes afraid that my father might take it upon himself to wash me, as he liked to do from time to time. I couldn't keep such words on me for long, because they tickled. When my mother soaked me, she was surprised to notice how dirty I was. I couldn't explain to her that the soap was washing away all the words that I had heard and collected that afternoon. Cleaned, I felt freed, and afterward ran around like a devil between the legs of all those women. I was afraid of slipping and falling. Clinging to those splayed thighs, I saw fleshy, hairy parts, a disgusting sight.

At night I went to sleep quickly, because I knew I would be visited by those images. I awaited them, armed with a whip, since I refused to see them so fat and ugly. I beat them, because I knew that I would never be like them. . . . An unacceptable ugliness. At night I hid myself and examined my belly with a small pocket mirror. My skin was white, soft to the touch, with no folds or wrinkles. At that time my mother examined me often. She didn't find anything, either! On the other hand, she was worried about my chest, which she bandaged with white linen, pulling the bands of cloth so tight I could hardly breathe. It was absolutely vital that no breasts should appear. I said nothing and submitted to her will.

At least my destiny had the advantage of being original and full of risk. I liked it that way. From time to time external signs confirmed me in this direction. The day, for example, when the cashier at the hammam refused to let me in, because she considered that I was no longer an innocent boy but already a young man capable by his mere presence of rousing the hidden desires of honest women! My mother made a show of protesting, but was really pleased. That evening she spoke proudly of it to my father, who decided to take me with him to the men's hammam in future. I was secretly delighted and awaited with enormous curiosity my entry into the male fog.

The men didn't talk much; they allowed themselves to be enveloped by the steam and washed themselves fairly quickly. A businesslike atmosphere reigned there. They quickly performed their ablutions, withdrew to a dark corner to shave their pubic hair, then left. I spent my time sitting around and deciphering the damp stones. There was nothing on them. The silence was interrupted by the noise of buckets being dropped or by the exclamations of certain men who got great pleasure out of being massaged. I later learned that in those dark corners the masseurs did other things than massage, that encounters and reunions took place there, and that the silence was not innocent.

I accompanied my father to his workshop. He explained to me how the business worked, introduced me to his employees and customers. He told them that I was the future. I said very little; the band of cloth around my chest was still very tight.

I went to the mosque. I enjoyed being in that huge building in which only men were admitted. I prayed all the time, often getting the words wrong. I enjoyed it all. The collective reading of the Koran made me feel dizzy. I lost my place and intoned anything that came into my head. I got great pleasure out of undermining all that fervor, mistreating the sacred text. My father took no notice of me. For him the important thing was my presence there.

It was there that I learned to be a dreamer. I examined the carved ceilings, the sentences written on them. These did not fall on my face; I rose to join them, scaling the column with the help of the Koranic chant. The verses lifted me fairly quickly to the top. I settled in the chandelier and observed the movement of the Arabic letters engraved in the plaster and wood. Then I set off on the back of a beautiful prayer:

If God gives you victory,
No one can defeat you.

I clung to the *alif* and let myself be pulled by the *nun*, which laid me in the arms of the *ba*. Thus I was taken, by all the letters, on a tour of the ceiling, and brought gently back to my starting point at the top of the column, where I fluttered down like a butterfly. I never disturbed the heads swaying to and fro as they read the Koran. I made myself very small and stuck close to my father, who was being gently lulled to sleep by the insistent rhythm of the reading. Afterward we all rushed out of the mosque, jostling one another. The men liked the struggle—the strongest got out first. I slipped out—I knew how to defend myself. My father told me that one must always defend oneself. On the way home, we bought curds in cloth, then stopped at the bakery to collect our bread. My father walked ahead. He liked to see me manage on my own. One day I was attacked by hooligans, who stole the bread basket from me. I couldn't fight: there were three of them. I went home in tears. My father gave me a blow that I remember to this day and said, "Stop crying! You're not a girl!" He was right—tears are very feminine! I dried my eyes and went out looking for hooligans to fight, but my father ran after me and brought me back into the house, saying that it was too late. . . .

Here I close the book. We leave childhood and move away from the Friday gate. I can no longer see it. I see the declining sun and your faces looking up at me. Day leaves us, night will scatter us. Let us go our separate ways and have the patience of the pilgrim!

4

The Saturday Gate

Friends, today we must move on. We are going to the third stage, the seventh day of the week, a market square, where grains are sold and peasants and animals sleep together, a place of exchange between town and country, surrounded by low walls and irrigated by a natural spring. I do not know what it holds in store for us. As we pass through the gate, we see sacks of wheat. I sold a donkey here once. The gate pierces the wall, a sort of ruin that leads nowhere. But we owe it a visit, partly out of superstition, partly out of a spirit of rigor. In principle, this gate corresponds to the stage of adolescence, a very obscure period. We have lost sight of our character's steps. He was taken in hand by his father and must have undergone difficult ordeals. It is a disturbed time, a time when the body is perplexed, hesitates, and gropes its way ahead. It is a period that we must imagine, a blank space left for the reader to fill in as he will.

"I think," says one reader, "it was the time when Ahmed,

aware of what was happening to him, underwent a profound crisis. I imagine him torn between the development of his body and his father's determination to make him wholly and entirely a man. . . ."

"I don't believe," says another, "there was a crisis. I think Ahmed developed according to his father's strategy. He had no doubts. He willingly took up the challenge. An intelligent child, he soon understood that this society of ours prefers men to women."

"No! What happened is simple enough. I know—I'm the oldest here. Perhaps even older than our revered master and storyteller, to whom I pay my heartfelt respects. I know this story. I don't need to guess or provide explanations. . . . Ahmed never left his father. He was educated outside the house, well away from the women. At school he learned to fight and fought often. His father encouraged him, but when he felt the boy's muscles, he found they were soft. Ahmed mistreated his sisters, who feared him. It was all quite normal! He was being prepared for the succession. In due course, he became a man. In any case, he was taught to behave like a man, at home as well as outside."

"But that doesn't take our story anywhere!"

"I will tell you the truth, if you will allow me: it's the story of a madman! If Ahmed had really existed, he would have ended up in a madhouse. . . . Since you say you have proof in this book you're hiding, why not hand it over? Then we'll see whether this story corresponds to the truth or whether you've made it all up just to waste our time and try our patience!"

The wind of rebellion blows among you! You are free to believe or not to believe this story. All I wanted was to

kindle your interest. As to what follows, I shall read it—
it is impressive. I open the book, I turn the blank pages.
. . . Listen!

There is a truth that cannot be told, not even suggested;
it can only be experienced in absolute solitude, surrounded
by a natural secrecy that is maintained effortlessly. Pain,
too, comes from depths that cannot be revealed. We do
not know whether those depths are in ourselves or elsewhere, in a graveyard, in a scarcely dug grave, only recently inhabited by withered flesh.

This truth, which is banal enough, unravels time and
the face, holds up a mirror to me in which I cannot see
myself without being overcome by a profound sadness—
not one of those youthful fits of melancholy that cradle
our pride and wrap us in nostalgia, but a sadness that
undermines one's whole being. The mirror has become
the route through which my body reaches that state, in
which it is crushed into the ground, digs a temporary
grave, and allows itself to be drawn by the living roots
that swarm beneath the stones. It is flattened beneath the
weight of that immense sadness which few people have
the privilege of knowing. So I avoid mirrors.

I haven't always been brave enough to betray myself—
that is to say, to descend the steps that my destiny has
traced out for me, which are leading me to the depths of
myself in the unbearable intimacy of a truth that cannot
be spoken. There only the wriggling worms keep me company. I am often tempted to organize my small inner cemetery in such a way that the sleeping shadows rise and
perform a dance around an erect male member that is mine.

I am both the shadow and the light that gives the
shadow birth. I am both the master of the house—a ruin

above a common grave—and its guest, the hand laid on the damp soil and the stone buried beneath a tuft of grass. I am both the gaze that sees itself and the mirror. Does my voice come from me, or is it that of the father who breathed it into me mouth to mouth as I slept? Sometimes I recognize it; sometimes I reject it. It is my finest, subtlest mask. The voice, deep, gravelly, does its work, intimidates me, and throws me into the crowd to show that I am worthy of it, that I bear it with confidence, naturally, without excessive pride, without anger or madness. I must master its rhythm, its timbre, its melody, and keep it in the warmth of my entrails.

The truth goes into exile. I have only to speak and the truth moves away, is forgotten; I become its gravedigger and disinterer. That is how the voice is: it does not betray me. And even if I wanted to betray it, reveal it in all its nakedness, I could not. I would not know how. I know its requirements: avoid anger, avoid tenderness, do not shout, do not whisper—in short, be ordinary. I am ordinary. And I trample underfoot the image that is unbearable to me. God, how heavy that truth weighs upon me! I am the architect and the house, the tree and the sap, a man and a woman. No detail must disturb the harshness of my task, whether from the outside or from the bottom of the grave. Not even blood.

One morning blood stained my sheets. Imprints of a fact about my body, rolled up in white linen, to shake the tiny certainty or give the lie to the architecture of appearance. On my thighs, a thin trickle of blood, an irregular pale-red line. Perhaps it was not blood but a swollen vein, a varicose vein colored by the night, a vision to disappear in the morning. Yet the sheet was damp, as if I had been trembling. It was certainly blood. The resistance of the body to the name—the splash from a belated circumcision. A reminder, a grimace of some buried memory, the memory of a life that I had not known and which could not be mine. It was strange being the bearer of a memory that had not been accumulated in time, in experience, but given unknown to all.

I felt the need to cure myself of myself, to unburden myself of my heavy solitude, which was like a wall receiving the complaints and cries of an abandoned horde, a mosque in the desert where people come at evening to lay down their sorrow and offer up a little of their blood. A quiet voice split the wall and told me that a dream can paralyze the morning stars. I looked at the sky and saw nothing but a white line traced with a perfect hand. I ought to lay a few stones on this path to mark my solitude.

That thin trickle of blood could only be a wound. My hand tried to stem the flow. I looked at my fingers, spread out, linked by a blob of that blood, and through them could see the garden, the motionless trees, and the sky broken by the highest branches. My heart hammered.

Yet I had been expecting it. Several times I had observed my mother and some of my sisters insert or remove pieces of white material between their legs. My mother cut up old sheets into pieces and kept them in the corner of a cupboard. My sisters used them without saying a word. I noticed everything and waited for the day when I, too, would open that cupboard secretly and put two or three layers of material between my legs. I would become a thief. At night I would watch for the trickle of blood. I would then examine the bloodstains on the material. That was the wound. A betrayal. My chest was still prevented from swelling. I imagined breasts growing inward, making breathing difficult. But I had no breasts. . . . That was one problem less. After the blood began, I was brought back to myself and the lines on my hand that destiny had drawn.

The Saturday gate closes on a great silence. With relief Ahmed passed through that door. He realized that his life was now a matter of keeping up appearances. It was no longer his father's will; it was his will.

5

Bab El Had

A tiny gate. One has to stoop to go through it. It stands
at the entrance of the medina and is linked with the one
at the other end, which is used for leaving. Actually this
is a false distinction: it depends where one is coming from.
But it is useful to know that throughout history there have
been gates for entering and gates for leaving. Ahmed would
often go back and forth between the two gates. He is now
twenty years of age, a cultivated young man, and his father
is thinking anxiously about his future. I suppose everybody
has been wondering what would happen in our story at
this crucial point. Here is how things turned out:

One day Ahmed went to see his father in his workshop
and said to him, "Father, what do you think of my voice?"

"It's fine, neither too deep nor too high-pitched."

"Good," Ahmed replied. "And what about my skin?"

"Your skin? Nothing unusual about it."

"Have you noticed that I don't shave every day?"

"Yes, why?"

"What do you think of my muscles?"

"Which muscles?"

"These, for example, the chest muscles?"

"I don't know."

"Have you noticed that it's hard here, on my chest? Father, I'm going to grow a mustache."

"Go ahead, if that's what you want to do!"

"From now on I'm going to wear a suit and tie."

"As you wish, Ahmed."

"Father! I'd like to get married."

"What? You're still too young."

"Didn't you marry young?"

"Yes, but things were different then. . . ."

"How are they now?"

"I don't know. You're embarrassing me."

"Isn't it a time of lies and mystification? Am I a human being or an image? A stone in a faded garden or a stout tree? Tell me, what am I?"

"Why all these questions?"

"I ask them so that you and I can face up to things. Neither of us is taken in. I don't just accept my condition and endure it, I actually like it. It is interesting. It gives me privileges that I would never have known. It opens doors for me, and I like that, even if it then locks me in a glass cage. Sometimes I nearly suffocate in my sleep. But when I wake, I am glad to be what I am. I've read all the books on anatomy, biology, psychology, and even astrology. I've read them and have decided to be fortunate. The miseries of solitude I will confine to a journal. By choosing life, I have accepted adventure. I'd like to pursue this story to the end. I'm a man. My name is Ahmed, according to the tradition of our Prophet. And I want a wife. We'll have a great but discreet festival to celebrate the engagement. Father, you've made me a man. I must remain one. And, as our beloved Prophet says, 'A complete Muslim is a married man.' "

The father was deeply disturbed. He did not know how to answer his son or what advice to give him. After all, Ahmed was merely carrying the situation to its logical conclusion. He had not told his father everything, for he had a plan. A long, uneasy silence ensued.

Ahmed became a petty tyrant. At home he made his sisters wait on him at lunch and dinner. He would shut himself up in the upper room. He abstained from any show of tenderness toward his mother, whom he seldom saw. At the workshop he had already begun to take the business in hand. Efficient, modern, cynical, he was an excellent dealer. His father couldn't keep up with him, so he let his son do as he wished. Ahmed had no friends. Secretive and domineering, he was feared. He sat in state in his room, went to bed late, and got up early. In fact he read a great deal and wrote through the night. Sometimes he would stay locked up in his room for four or five days on end. Only his mother dared knock at his door. He coughed rather than speak, just to indicate that he was still alive.

One day he summoned his mother and said to her in a firm voice, "I have chosen the woman who will be my wife."

The mother had already been warned of her son's intentions by her husband. She said nothing, betrayed not the slightest surprise. Nothing her son ever did or said could shock her any more. She told herself that madness had got into his brain. She dared not think that he had become a monster. The past year his behavior had changed out of all recognition. He had become odd, to say the least, sometimes destructive and violent. She looked up at him and said, "Who is she?"

"Fatima."

"Fatima?"

"My cousin, the daughter of my uncle, my father's younger brother, he who rejoiced at the birth of each of your daughters."

"But you can't. Fatima is ill—she's an epileptic and has a limp. . . ."

"Precisely!"

"You're a monster."

"I'm your son, no more, no less."

"You'll bring unhappiness on us all!"

"I'm only obeying you, you and my father. You marked out a path for me: I've taken it, followed it, and, out of curiosity, I've gone a little farther.

"In this family the women wrap themselves in a shroud of silence. They obey. My sisters obey. You keep quiet and I give the orders. How ironic! How have you managed not to breathe the slightest seed of discontent into your daughters? They come and go, slinking along the walls, awaiting the providential husband. . . . What a miserable existence! Have you seen my body? It's grown—it's come home. I've shed the other bark—it was fragile and transparent. My body has grown and I no longer sleep in another's body. I lie on the edge of your shroud. You say nothing. You're right. I'll tell you something else. Certain verses of the Koran that I had to learn by heart have come back into my mind recently, just like that, for no apparent reason. They go through my head, stop for a second, then vanish: 'God charges you, concerning your children: to the male the like of the portion of two females. . . .' So, I'm expecting to get married and to start a home, a hearth. My house will be a glass cage—not much, just a room lined with mirrors, which will reflect the light and images. First I must get engaged. But we don't have to rush things. For the time being I'm going to write, perhaps love poems for the sacrificial woman—her or me. I'll leave the choice to you."

O my companions! This character eludes our grasp. To my way of thinking, he should not have become cruel. It seems to me that he has given us the slip. That sudden, brutal change of mind disturbs me, and I don't know where it will lead. He is damned, weighed down by a curse, transformed by witches. Do you think, you who listen to me, that he is an unscrupulous man, a monster? A monster who writes poems! I doubt it, and I feel unhappy with this face. I come back to the book. The ink is pale; drops of water—perhaps tears—have made this page illegible. I find it difficult to read:

In the aching arms of my body I hold myself; I descend to the depths as if to escape myself. I let myself slip into a wrinkle; I love the smell of that valley. I startle at the cry of the mare sent by the absent one. She is white and I cover my eyes. Slowly my body opens to my desire. I take it by the hand. It resists. The mare gallops off. I fall asleep, entwined in my arms.

Is it the sea that murmurs thus in the ear of a dead horse? Is it a horse or a siren?

What ritual of shipwreck is dragged down by the sea's hair? I am shut up in an image, and the tall waves pursue me. I fall, I faint. Is it possible to faint in sleep, to lose consciousness and no longer recognize the feel of familiar objects? I have built my house with shifting images. I am not playing; I am trying not to die. I have at least the whole of my life to answer a question: Who am I? And who is the other? A gust of wind at dawn? A motionless landscape? A trembling leaf? A coil of white smoke above a mountain?

I write all these words and I hear the wind, not outside, but inside my head. A strong wind, it rattles the shutters through which I enter the dream. I see that a door is leaning to one side. Will it fall where I rest my head to welcome other lives, to stroke other faces? They are gloomy faces and gay ones, but I love them because I invent them. I make them very different from my own, whether distorted or sublime, snatched from the light of day and stuck on the branches of the tree like a witch's conquests.

Sometimes the winter of those faces chills my blood. I leave them, go and look elsewhere. I take hands. I choose large, delicate ones. I shake them, kiss them, suck them. I become intoxicated. Hands resist me less. They cannot make grimaces. Faces take revenge on my freedom by grimacing the whole time. That is why I set them aside. Not violently, but I set them aside; I pile them up. They are crushed. They suffer. Some even cry out, hooting like owls, mewling, gnashing their teeth. In different faces. Neither men's nor women's, but faces of absolute beauty. The hands betray me, too, especially when I try to match them with the faces.

The main thing is to avoid shipwreck. The ritual of shipwreck obsesses me. I run the risk of losing everything, and I have no desire to find myself outside again, with the others. My nakedness is my sublime privilege. I am the only one to observe it. I am the only one to curse it. I dance. I turn and turn. I clap my hands. I strike the ground with my feet. I lean toward the trap door behind which I hide my creatures. I am afraid of falling and confuse myself with one of those unsmiling faces. I turn and turn till I'm dizzy. The sweat stands out on my forehead. My body dances to some African rhythm. . . . I'm in the bush and mingle with the naked men. I forget to ask myself who I am. I aspire to the silence of the heart. I am tracked down and give my mouth to a flame in the forest.

I'm not in Africa, but in a cemetery by the sea. I feel cold. All the graves have been emptied, abandoned. The wind that whistles through is their prisoner. A horse painted with the blues of night gallops through this cemetery. My eyes fall out and are stuck in the horse's head. The darkness swallows me up. I feel safe. I am caught by warm hands. They stroke my back. I guess whose they are. They are not mine. I lack everything and recoil. Is it tiredness or the idea of going back to myself and to the house? I would like to laugh, because I know that, condemned to isolation, I will not be able to overcome fear. It is said that this is what anxiety is.

I have spent years adapting to my solitude. My reclusion is willed, chosen, loved. Moreover, I shall get faces and hands from it, journeys and poems. Out of suffering I am building a palace in which death will have no place. Though I will not repulse it, it will be forbidden entry. But suffering is sufficient unto itself; there is no need to deliver a mighty blow. This body is made up of fibers that accumulate pain and intimidate death. That is my freedom. Anxiety withdraws, and I am left alone to fight until dawn. At daybreak I drop with exhaustion and joy. The others understand nothing. They are unworthy of my madness.

Such are my nights—enchanted. I also like to set them high on the rocks and wait for the wind to shake them, wash them, separate them from sleep, shake off the darkness from them, undress them, and bring them to me wrapped in nothing but a cloud of dreams. Then everything becomes limpid. I forget. I sink gently into the other's open body.

I no longer ask anybody anything. I drink coffee and live. Neither good nor evil. I ask nobody anything: my questions have no answers. I know this, because I can see both sides of the mirror. I am not really very serious. I like to play, even if I have to hurt people. I have been above evil for a long time now, looking at all that from afar, from the heights of my solitude. It is strange—my sternness, my harshness opens up doors for me. I don't ask so much! I jostle everybody. I ask not for love, but for abandonment. They don't understand. Hence the need to live my condition in all its horror.

Today I am pleased to think of the woman who will become my wife. I don't speak of desire yet; I speak of servitude. She will come, dragging one leg, her face contorted, her eyes anxious, overcome by my request. I shall have her brought up to my room and talk to her of my nights. I shall kiss her hand, say that she is beautiful; I shall make her cry and let her indulge her feelings. I shall observe her, struggling against death, slobbering, imploring. I shall kiss her on the forehead; she will calm down again, then set off for home without looking back.

I am not depressed, I am exasperated. I am not sad, I am desperate. My night has given me nothing. It has passed, unperceived, calm, empty, dark.

Friends, I told you this gate was narrow. I read on your faces embarrassment and anxiety. This confession both enlightens us and distances us. It makes the character even more strange.

Certain very obscure exchanges of letters were to upset our hero's plans and life. These letters, entrusted to the notebook, are not all dated, but in reading them one may well place them at this point in our story. Either they are not signed or the signature is absolutely illegible. Sometimes it consists of a cross, sometimes initials or arabesques.

Are they from an anonymous correspondent? Or are they imaginary? Or did he write to himself in his isolation?

The first letter does not appear in the notebook—it must have been lost. The next is a reply to it:

So it seems that my punishment will be life itself! Your letter did not surprise me. I guessed how you were able to procure the strange private details of my life. The way in which you slip yourself into those questions, the imprudence with which you interfere in my dream, makes you an accomplice of whatever I may commit or provoke by way of misfortune. Your signature is an illegible scribble. The letter is not dated. Are you by any chance the exterminating angel? If you are, come see me—we might have a good laugh together. . . . *Poste restante!* Initials! So much mystery . . .

I found your letter under the stone at the entrance to the garden. Thank you for answering. You are still being very evasive. I have been waiting for you a long time. My questions were probably not very precise. But, you see, I cannot reveal my identity without incurring danger that would bring misfortune on both of us. Our correspondence must remain confidential. I am depending on your sense of secrecy.

The purpose that guides me and has brought me to you is stamped with the seal of the impossible. Yet I like walking on that path; I am patient, my hopes nourished by the dream I have of you whenever the fever rises, when I see you without your seeing me, as you talk to yourself or lie down naked in the white pages of this notebook. I observe you and follow you till you're out of breath; it's amazing how much you move, how much you tear around. I would like to be able to stop you for a moment, a brief instant, to look at your eyes and their lids. But I have only a vague image of you—and maybe it's better that way!

Since you have come to my house to spy on me and observe my gestures and thoughts, I have decided to do a little housework. My room is not very large. The parallel mirrors, the roof light, the large windows, and my solitude make it seem larger than it is. I am going to make it even larger by cleaning up my life and my memories, for there is nothing more cumbersome than things left by time in some floor of the memory. (People say "a corner of the memory," but I know that it is a floor, for there are so many other objects piled up waiting for a sign to tumble down and encumber my present life.) On your next visit you will be surprised—you may not even recognize the place. I do not conceal the fact that I am trying to bring about your ruin. You will fall into the net of your boldness, or into a ditch by the roadside. But let us stay together for a while. Let us not lose sight of each other. Let me hear from you soon!

Not having the time to come see you and being unsure whether my presence would disturb you, I still prefer to write you.

I have learned that you have expressed the wish and determination to marry. A fine gesture, in principle. But your soul seems to be wandering. Will you dare make a victim of some poor, defenseless creature? No! That would be unworthy of you. However, if you wish to do harm to one of your uncles, I may have a few ideas to offer you. But I remain convinced that your genius has ambitions of much wider scope!

I shall still remain in the shadow of an anonymity that may lead anywhere, especially to you, to your thoughts, to your soul, to your body lying next to mine. . . .

My father is ill. I must give up all my plans. I feel it's a difficult time. I am obsessed by the idea of his disappearance. It pains me to hear him cough. My mother does not seem to be prepared for this ordeal. I leave my room and lie beside him, without sleeping. I observe the rhythm of his breathing. I watch over him and quietly weep over myself.

Today I am telling you of my fear and pain, but you are ensconced in anonymity, which brings me close to you. I would not like to see your face or hear your voice. Let me guess what you are like through your letters. Do not be angry with me if I am slow to give you news of myself.

43

The exchange of letters breaks off here to make room for the major event, the decisive ordeal, the most important turning point in our character's life. The father's death was to be preceded by a number of incidents, plottings, and schemings, which were to strengthen the heir's resolve and give his status an unchallenged legitimacy. Bab El Had, as its name suggests, is the outer gate, the wall erected to put an end to a situation. It will be our last gate, for it was closed against us without warning. I spoke to you, I know, of seven gates, and now I do not know where the story is leading. It does not stop at this gate, but it will no longer go through gates pierced in a wall. It will go around and around a circular street, and we will have to follow it with ever more attention.

6

The Forgotten Gate

We must now slip through breaches in the wall, the forgotten openings; we must walk on tiptoe and prick up our ears, not during the day, but at evening, when the moon gives shade to our story, when the stars are gathering in the corner of the sky and observe the world as it falls into sleep.

O my friends, in your company I dare not speak of God, the indifferent, the supreme. I remember some words spoken by a great writer that still intrigue me: "We do not know where God places his accents, and life is as discreet as a crime." We are its slaves, and we are dropping with exhaustion. As for me, I am the blind man dancing on an edge; at any moment I may fall. That is what adventure is—a few commas holding us back.

The father died, slowly. Death took its time and gathered him up one morning, in his sleep. Ahmed took things in hand, with authority. He summoned his seven sisters and told them more or less the following: "From this day on, I'm no longer your brother; I'm not your father, either, but your guardian. I have the duty and the right to watch over you. You owe me obedience and respect. Anyway, I don't have to remind you that I'm a man of order and that if in our house women are inferior to men it's not because God wishes it or because the prophets decided it thus, but because the women accept this fate. So submit, and live in silence!"

After this statement of intent, he summoned the notaries, invited his uncles, and settled the question of the inheritance. Order reigned. Ahmed received from his anonymous correspondent a short letter of condolence to which he replied a few days later:

My father's imprint still lies on my body. He may be dead, but I know he will come back. Some evening he will come down the hillside and open the city gates one by one. I feel no sorrow. My pain is outside of me, my eyes are dry, and my innocence is stained by a little pus. I see myself smeared with this yellowish liquid, which reminds me of the time and place of death.

Now I am master of the house. My sisters are resigned to it. Their blood moves sluggishly. My mother has withdrawn into the silence of mourning. And I am beset by doubts: I do not know what object, what garden, what night I shall bring back from the future. I never fall asleep without walking along several dark, unknown paths. They are traced by a familiar hand—perhaps my father's—on a white page, bare and deserted, which even the wind avoids. That is the future, a veiled statue walking alone through that white expanse, a territory of unbearable light.

See you soon.

Must I remind you, you who may not exist, that I am incapable of friendship and still less of love?

P.S. Each morning, on rising, I look out the window to see whether the sky has not slipped while I was asleep and washed into the inner courtyard of the house. I am convinced that one day, sooner or later, it will descend to burn my remains.

While the storyteller was reading this letter, a tall, thin man kept pacing back and forth, moving to the center of the circle, then around it, waving a stick as if he wanted to protest or speak up to correct something. Finally he stood in the middle, keeping the storyteller at a distance with his cane, and addressed the crowd:

This man is hiding the truth from you. He is afraid to tell you everything. It was I who told him this story. It is a terrible story. I did not invent it. I lived through it. I belong to the man's family. I am the brother of Fatima, Ahmed's wife, or, rather, the woman who plays the role of wife, but a wife who allowed herself to be swept up into a perversion that is too complicated for us good, simple Muslims. When his mother came, surrounded by her seven daughters, to deliver a large bouquet of flowers to the house, and then came her servants, laden with presents, she whispered into my mother's ear some such words as "The same blood that bound us together in the past will unite us once again, God willing."

After the gestures and words of welcome, she spoke slowly, syllable by syllable, the name of Fa-ti-ma, repeating it several times lest there be any confusion. My mother stopped smiling. To ask for the hand in marriage of the wretched Fatima, with her limp and her epileptic fits, was either too good a stroke of fortune or an insult.

As soon as her name was spoken, she was taken away and shut up in the upper room, and no one said anything —either yes or no. They were waiting to consult the father.

Relations between the two families had never been good—jealousy and rivalry nourished a petty, silent war— but appearances were kept up. This is what some call hypocrisy. The two brothers were not very fond of each other, and each wife obviously took her husband's part. In fact, the men secretly hated each other, and the women took it upon themselves to keep the tension going. They would say spiteful little things to each other when they met at the baths or at home. No one would have imagined that one day the two families would be united in marriage.

The father hesitated: he suspected that Ahmed's gesture must conceal some secret motive. Moreover, he found Ahmed, whom he saw very seldom, extremely intriguing. He had confused ideas about that individual—anyway, he was furious with himself for thinking ill of anyone. He said a prayer to God for justice to be done. All his life he had been counting on that inheritance. With the arrival of Ahmed, he was forced to bury those hopes; he felt that he was a victim of some injustice of fate or some scheme of destiny. At first he rejected the proposal of marriage out of hand. Then he came around to the idea of talking about it with Fatima. She wanted to marry. In the end he gave in.

Ahmed laid down his conditions: the two families would remain apart; he would live alone with his wife. She would leave the house only to go to the baths or to the hospital. He was thinking of taking her to consult certain great doctors, of getting her cured, giving her a chance. As he spoke, he concealed his true face behind a firm manner. He said things they did not entirely understand—philosophical reflections, thoughts on this and that. I remember it very well, because the end of his speech intrigued me and disturbed me greatly. He said: "A lonely passenger from the absolute, I cling to my outer skin in this forest thick with lies. I stand behind a wall of glass or crystal and observe the commerce of others. They are small, and they stoop under so much weight. For a long time now I have laughed at myself and at that other who is now talking to you, whom you think you see and hear. I am talking to myself, and I fear you will be lost in this flurry of stammered words. You will have news of me on the exact day of my death. It will be a splendid, sunny day, the day when the bird inside me will sing. . . ." We thought his mind was beginning to wander, that all his reading was driving him insane. He spoke without interruption and some of what he said was inaudible, since he stuck his head into his jellaba, as if he were praying or communicating some secret to an invisible person.

You cannot imagine, my friends, what happened next. Our storyteller is pretending to read from a book that Ahmed is supposed to have left behind him. That is untrue! Of course the book exists, but it is not that old notebook, yellowed by the sun, which our storyteller has covered with that dirty scarf. Anyway, it isn't a notebook, but a cheap edition of the Koran. It's very peculiar—he looks at the verses and reads the diary of a madman, a victim of his own illusions. Bravo! What courage, what deception!

I am the one who has Ahmed's diary—as you might expect. I stole it the day after his death. Here it is. It is covered with a newspaper of the time. You can read the date—does it not coincide with that of his death? Our storyteller is very talented! What he has read to us is unworthy of inclusion in this notebook.

Companions! Don't go away, listen to me. I belong to this story. I am climbing this wooden ladder. Be patient! Wait until I have reached the top of the terrace. I am scaling the walls of the house. I am going to sit on a mat on the white terrace, and open the book to tell you the strange and beautiful story of Fatima, who was touched by grace, and of Ahmed, cloistered in the vapors of evil. The story of virtue pierced to the heart by so many poisoned arrows. Companions, gather around. Don't rush—don't trample over our storyteller. Let him go. Climb the ladders and pay attention to the wind, rise, scale the outer walls, prick up your ears, open your eyes, and let us set out together, not on a carpet or on a cloud, but on a thick layer of colorful musical words and sentences. This song that you hear was one of Ahmed's favorites. It comes from far off, from the South, over the high mountains. A sad song, it is like the earth gently raising its great stones one by one and bringing to our ears the wounded sounds emitted by a trampled body.

You are silent, and your faces are grave. Ah, I see our old storyteller is coming back. He is sitting down among you. Welcome! I am merely continuing your story. Perhaps I upset you. Excuse my gestures of impatience. It is the song that has brought you back. It brings us all back to the earth. Come closer, come closer to me. You will be able to intervene in this story, if you wish. Now I shall read from Ahmed's diary, which opens, or continues—I know not—with these words: "The days are stones; they pile up one on top of another. . . ."

It is the confession of a wounded man—he is quoting from a Greek poet.

7

The Walled-up Gate

Two old women, gray and shriveled, with gloomy looks and curt, precise gestures, accompanied Fatima. Quietly, with no sign of celebration, they were to hand over to me the woman who was to carry out the role of wife in my home. She was wrapped in a white jellaba. Her eyes were lowered, and even if she had dared to look up, the two women would have stopped her. That's modesty for you! Not looking a man in the eye, as a sign of submission; it's done out of duty, seldom out of respect or because of affection. The two women held her tight, each holding one arm. They were hurting her. They were walking quickly, propelling her forward, with decisive steps.

But she had decided nothing. She couldn't even dream of love. She didn't want to share those illusions. Her body betrayed her, deserting her in the fullness of youth. The demons of the beyond often visited her, slipping into her blood, disturbing it, making it circulate too quickly or in an irregular way. Her blood would disturb her breathing, and she would faint and fall. Her body moved away, far from her consciousness. It was given to uncontrolled gesticulations, as if fighting itself, as if fighting the wind or the demons. She was left alone to untangle the threads of all those knots. Slowly her body came back to her, resumed its place, exhausted, beaten pain-ridden.

Lying stretched out on the ground to rest, she thanked God for giving her back the power to breathe normally, to get up and go run in the street. Everybody in the family had got used to seeing her knock her head against invisible walls. Nobody bothered or worried about it. The most anyone ever said was "Well! That fit was worse than the one last week. It must be the heat!" She was left alone to have her fit, so she didn't disturb anything: her brothers and sisters were left undisturbed, full of the future, happy to be able to make plans, annoyed at not having enough money to go out in society more, put out at having a sister who introduced a false note into so harmonious a landscape.

In the end, Fatima had her own space—an uncomfortable room, near the terrace. They often forgot about her. Two or three times, I found her crying for no apparent reason, perhaps to forget or just to pass the time. She was very bored, and since nobody in her family showed her the slightest kindness, she sank into a shroud of pitiful melancholy. Sacrificed and exhausted, she was a tiny thing laid by mistake or by some curse on the everyday monotony of a narrow existence, laid on a table left in a corner of the courtyard where the cats leap and twist and turn, trying to catch flies.

Was she beautiful? I still wonder even today. It has to

be admitted that her face got lined at an early age, marked by the frequent and increasingly violent fits. Her features had kept little of their delicacy, though a soft, gentle light glowed in her fair eyes. She had a small nose, and her cheeks were covered with the eternal spots of youth. What I could not like was her mouth, which twisted during the fits and wore a permanent grimace, like an enormous comma on a white page. Her body was firm, despite her short right leg. Firm and hard. Her breasts were small, with a few hairs around the nipples. When I took her in my arms, not to express sexual desire but to console her for her distress, I felt that body, reduced to an active skeleton, fighting with ghosts. It felt hot, nervous, determined to conquer in order to live, to breathe normally, to be able to run and dance, swim and climb, like a tiny star on the foam of tall, beautiful waves. I felt it struggling against death with all the means at its disposal: nerves and blood. She often had hemorrhages. She would then say that her blood was angry, that it was not worth keeping, that it was good for nothing. She didn't want to have a child, though her dreams were peopled by hordes of brats. As she lay asleep at my side, she would cling to my arm, sucking her thumb, her body relaxed and calm.

On the day of her arrival in my house, she whispered in my ear as if confiding a secret: "Thank you for getting me out of the other house. We will be brother and sister. You have my soul and my heart, but my body belongs to the earth and the devil that laid it waste." She went to sleep shortly afterward, and I stayed alone, reflecting on her stammered words. I began to have doubts about myself and my appearance. Did she know about me? Did she want to forestall the speech that I had prepared in my head to

54

warn her without revealing my secrets to her? Strange! In the end I came to the conclusion that for a long time she had simply suppressed all sexuality in herself and had accepted this marriage in the belief that I had asked for it not out of love but simply as a social arrangement, to conceal some infirmity or perversion. She must have thought I was a homosexual, needing a cover to silence the gossips, or impotent and wanting to keep up appearances. That way I would have spent my life playing with appearances, all appearances—even those that may have been the truth fabricated for me.

I didn't mind—her boldness made things easier. I gave her a bed next to mine and busied myself with her as much as I could. She never undressed in front of me; nor did I in front of her. Modesty and chastity reigned in our large room. One day, as she lay asleep, I tried to see if she had been circumcised or if the lips of her vagina had been sewed up. I gently lifted the sheet and found that she was wearing a strong girdle around her pelvis, like a steel chastity belt, to discourage desire—or to provoke it, and destroy it, all the more.

Fatima's presence disturbed me greatly. At first I liked the difficulty and complexity of the situation. Then I began to lose patience. I was no longer master of my world and my solitude. That wounded creature at my side, that intrusion that I had myself installed inside my secret, private life, that grave, desperate woman who was no longer a woman, who had traveled a painful path, that woman who didn't even aspire to be a man, but to be nothing at all, that woman who almost never spoke, murmuring a sentence or two from time to time, but enclosing herself in a long silence, reading books of mysticism, and sleeping without making the slightest sound, that woman prevented me from sleeping.

Sometimes I observed her for a long time in her sleep, staring at her until the features and contours of her face became blurred and I penetrated that dark, shadowy pit in which her deepest thoughts were kept. Silently I pursued my delusion, successfully reaching her thoughts as if I myself had expressed them. That was my mirror, my weakness; that is what haunted me. I heard her steps in the middle of the night, moving slowly over an old, creaking floor. In fact it wasn't a wooden floor, but I imagined the sound and the sound conjured up a floor made of old wood that had come from some ruined house, abandoned by travelers in a hurry; the house was an old hut in a wood, surrounded by oaks that had been ravaged by time. I climbed up onto one of the few safe branches and looked down at the shed, at the leaky roof, which let in the light and through which I could see the traces of footprints in the dust. These led me to a cave where rats and other beasts, whose names I do not know, live happily. In that cave, a veritable prehistoric grotto, lay the thoughts of the woman who was asleep in the same room as I, and whom I regarded with mixed feelings of pity, tenderness, and anger, a whirlpool in which I was losing the sense of things and patience with them, in which I was becoming more and more a stranger to my destiny and my projects. That presence, however silent; that weight, sometimes light, sometimes heavy; that difficult breathing, that thing that scarcely moved, that inscrutable gaze, that girdled belly, that absent sex, denied, refused, that creature lived only to flail about in her epileptic fits and to touch with her fingers the delicate, imprecise face of death, then to return to the cave and her thoughts. These were neither sad nor happy, simply thrown in shreds into a sack—the rats had tried to eat them but must have given up, because they were smeared with a toxic substance that protected them and kept them intact.

She slept a great deal; when she was awake, she shut herself away for long periods in the bathroom, gave a few orders to the maid, then returned to her isolation. She never mixed with my sisters, accepted no invitation; in the evening, when I came home, she muttered a few words of thanks as if she owed me something.

My sisters never understood the meaning of this marriage. My mother dared not speak to me about it. And I occupied myself as much as possible with the business, which my father had left in a fairly bad state.

Gradually I was overcome by scruples—and insomnia. I wanted to get rid of Fatima in some way that would not harm her. I put her in a room well removed from mine. Yet I came to hate her. I realized I had failed in the process that I had planned and set in motion. Because she was handicapped, that woman turned out to be stronger, harder, more unbending than I could have foreseen. Though I had intended to use her to perfect my social appearance, it was she who had managed to use me; she almost dragged me into her profound despair.

I write that but I'm not sure of the words, because I don't know the whole truth. That woman had a special kind of intelligence. All the words she never spoke, all the words she saved up, were poured into her unshakable condition, reinforcing her plans and projects. She had already given up living and was moving slowly and surely toward disappearance, toward extinction. Not a sudden death, but a slow series of backward steps toward the gaping ditch behind the horizon. She no longer took her medicines, ate little, spoke hardly at all.

She wanted not only to die but to drag me down with her as well. At night she would come into my room and cling to my bed, just before the fit took her. She would pull on my arm until I fell down at her side or throttle me with all her strength, in an attempt to rid herself of the demons rushing around inside her. Each time it lasted a little longer. I no longer knew how to react or how to avoid these painful scenes. She said I was her only support, the only creature she loved, and wanted me to accompany her in each of her falls. I did not really understand until the night she slipped into my bed as I slept and began gently to stroke my stomach. I woke up with a start and violently pushed her away. I was furious. She smiled for the first time, but her smile did not reassure me. I could not bear it. I wanted her to die. I was furious with her for being sick, for being a woman, for being there, by my will, my cruelty, my calculation, and my hatred of myself.

One evening, her eyes already fixed on the trap door of darkness, her face serene but very pale, her tiny body crouching in the corner of the bed, her hands cold and softer than usual, she said to me, with a little smile: "I have always known who you are, and that is why, my sister, my cousin, I have come to die here, near you. We were both born leaning over the stone at the bottom of the dry well, over infertile ground, surrounded by unloving looks. We are women before being sick, or perhaps we are sick because we are women. . . . I know our wound; we share it. I am going. . . . I am your wife and you are mine. . . . You will be a widower and I . . . Let's say I was a mistake. Not a very serious one, just a minor deviation from the course that was never rectified . . . Oh, I'm talking too much—I'm going out of my mind! Good night. See you one day!"

8

The Houseless Woman

And so he became a widower. Friends, this episode in his life was painful, disturbing, and incomprehensible.

"No, it was quite logical!" said a member of the audience. "He used that poor invalid to reassure himself and to strengthen his personality. It reminds me of another story, something that happened at the end of the last century in the south of the country. Allow me to tell it to you quickly. It's the story of a warrior chieftain, a terrible creature named Antar. He was a pitiless leader, a brute, with a terrible reputation that went beyond clan and frontiers. He commanded his men without shouting, without making violent gestures. All he had to do was give orders in a quiet voice, contrasting with the words he spoke, and he was never disobeyed. He had his own army, and resisted the occupiers without ever challenging the central authority. Feared and respected, he tolerated no weakness or faintheartedness in his men, ruthlessly pursued and punished the corrupt, and wielded his own power and justice, which were never arbitrary; his strictness was unwavering, his ideas were never compromised; in short, he was an exemplary man of legendary courage, that man, that secretive, Antar, who slept with his rifle by his side. Yet the day he died it was discovered that all that terror, all that strength resided in a woman's body. A mausoleum was erected to him on the spot where he died. Today he is regarded as a saint. He is the Marabout of wanderers, venerated by all those who run away, who leave their homes because they are eaten up by doubt, seeking the inner face of the truth. . . ."

At this point the storyteller intervened, saying with a smile: "Yes, my friend, I, too, know that story. It happened perhaps a hundred years ago. It is the story of the 'isolated leader,' a figure who fascinated all those who came near him. Sometimes he would turn up veiled; his troops thought he wanted to surprise them, but in fact he was offering his nights to a young man of rough beauty, a sort of wandering bandit who always carried a dagger, either to defend himself or to take his own life if necessary. He lived in a cave and spent his time smoking kief and awaiting the beauty of his nights. Of course he never knew that this woman was a woman only in her body, only in his arms. She offered him money; he refused it. She told him which places to burgle and guaranteed him maximum security, then disappeared, only to reappear unexpected one starlit night. They said little to each other, mingling their bodies and preserving their souls. It is said that one night they fought, because, as they made love, she gained the upper position after forcing him to lie on his belly, and simulated sodomy. Though the man yelled with rage, she pinned him down with all her strength, immobilizing him, pressing his face into the ground. When he managed to get free, he grabbed his dagger, but, quicker than he, she leaped on him and threw him to the ground. As he fell, the weapon grazed his arm. He began to weep. She spat in his face, kicked him in the balls, and left. It was over. She never came back, and the wounded bandit went mad, left his cave, and took to haunting the entrances of mosques, sick with love and hate. He must have got lost in the crowd or been swallowed up in an earthquake. As for our leader, he died young, without suffering any illness, in his sleep. When they undressed him to wash him and wrap him in his shroud, you can imagine the amazement; they discovered that it was a woman, whose beauty suddenly appeared as the essence of that hidden truth, as the riddle that swung between excessive darkness and light.

"This story has traveled to different countries and times. It has come down to us today somewhat transformed. Isn't that the destiny of all stories that circulate and trickle down from the highest sources? They live longer than men and bring beauty to our days."

"But what became of our hero after Fatima's death?" someone asked.

He became sad, sadder than before, for his whole life was like flesh subjected to repeated changes of skin, to the need to make himself mask upon mask. He withdrew to his room, delegated the management of his business to a man who was faithful to the family, and began to write confused, unreadable things. It was at this point that he began once again to receive letters from his anonymous correspondent. Those letters are there, with the same fine, careful, secretive handwriting; that distant voice, never named, helped him to live and reflect upon his condition. He developed an intimate relationship with that correspondent; at last he could speak, exist in his truth, live without a mask, in a certain freedom, however limited and subject to surveillance, even with joy, if an inward, silent joy. This is the letter he received after Fatima's death.

Thursday, April 8. Friend, I know, I feel the wound you bear within you, and I knew the mourning of your days well before the death of that poor girl. You believe yourself capable of every cruelty, beginning with those that slashed your body and darkened your days. Out of pride or ambition, you have summoned up misfortune, even in your most private life, and you have turned it not into a pleasure, but into a dangerous game in which you have lost the skin of one of your masks. You wanted that union, not out of pity, but out of revenge. There you made a mistake, and your intelligence has sunk into maneuvers unworthy of your ambitions. Allow me to tell you, as a friend, in all frankness, what I feel. This situation would be too much for most people to bear, but I don't think it will be for you. The girl was a lost soul and had begun her fall long before. What is the point now of isolating yourself in that room, surrounded by books and candles? Why not go out into the street, abandoning masks and fear? I say this, knowing you are suffering. I have known and observed you for a long time now. I have learned to read your heart, and your melancholy reaches me despite the distance between us and the impossibility of our ever meeting. What are you going to turn your mind to now? You know how unjust our society is with women, how our religion favors men. You know that, in order to live according to one's own wishes and desires, one must have power. You have required a taste for privileges, and, perhaps without wishing it, you have ignored and despised your sisters. They hate you and await only your departure. You will have failed to show due love and respect to your mother, a good woman who has done nothing but obey you all your life. She still waits and hopes for your return, your return to her breast, your return to her love. Since her husband's death, madness and silence have ravaged her and you have forgotten her. She is dying from your desertion. She is losing her hearing and her sight. She awaits you.

I, too, await you, but I have more patience. I have enough reserves of love in me for you and your destiny. . . . Till the next time, your friend!

This letter annoyed him. He felt that he was being judged and harshly criticized. He was tempted to break off the correspondence, but a desire to understand and explain what was happening inside him overcame his silence and pride.

Saturday, at night. Your last letter disturbed me. For a long time I hesitated before replying. But, after all, you must be more than a confidant, a witness of my solitude. Solitude is my choice and my territory. I inhabit it like a wound lodged in my body that refuses to heal. I say "inhabit it," but, on reflection, it is solitude, with its terrors, its heavy silences, and its invading impotence, that has chosen me as its territory, as a peaceful home in which happiness has the taste of death. I know I must live there without hoping for anything; time transforms and strengthens that obligation. I would like to say it's a question that goes beyond notions of duty or mood. You may understand that one day, if our faces ever meet.

Since I withdrew to my room, I have been progressing over the sands of a desert where I see no way out, where the horizon is little more than a blue, ever-receding line; I dream of crossing that blue line and walking through an endless steppe, without thought of what might happen. . . . I walk in order to divest myself of things, to cleanse myself, to rid myself of a question that haunts me and of which I never speak—desire. I am tired of carrying its insinuations in my body, without being able either to reject them or to make them mine. I shall remain profoundly unconsoled, with a face that is not mine and a desire that I cannot name.

Finally, I would like to say why your letter has discouraged me: suddenly you become moralizing. As you know, I hate psychology and anything that encourages guilt. I thought Muslim fatalism (does it exist?) would spare us that petty, evil-smelling emotion. If I write to you, if I have agreed to keep up this epistolary dialogue with you, it is not to be subjected to social morality. The great, the huge ordeal through which I am passing has meaning only outside those petty, psychological schemata that claim to know and explain why a woman is a woman and a man a man. No, my friend, the family, as it exists in our countries, with the all-powerful father and the women relegated to domesticity, with a portion of authority left them by the male, that family I reject, wrap up in mist, and no longer recognize.

I shall stop here, for I feel anger rising within me and

I cannot allow myself the luxury of allowing to cohabit in the same wound the distress that makes me live and the anger that denatures my deepest thoughts, my sense of purpose. I now leave you and return to my reading. Perhaps tomorrow I shall open the window. I hope to hear from you very soon, friend of my solitude!

Friends, I close the book here, open up my heart, and appeal to my reason. During that period of retirement, no one saw him. He had shut himself up in the upper room and communicated with the outside by means of little notes that were often illegible or strange. His mother could not read. She refused to join in this game and threw away the notes addressed to her. He almost never wrote to his sisters, three of whom no longer lived in the big house. They had married and seldom visited their sick mother.

Ahmed reigned even while absent and invisible. His presence was felt and feared in the house. Everybody spoke quietly for fear of disturbing him. He stayed up there, no longer went out, and only old Malika, the maid who had witnessed his birth and for whom he felt some tenderness, was allowed to push open his door and tend him. She brought him food—she even snitched wine and kief for him—and cleaned his room and the small adjacent bathroom. When she came in, she covered herself entirely with a sheet and sat on a chair on the tiny balcony that overlooked the old town. On leaving, she hid the empty wine bottles in a bag and muttered a few prayers, such as "May Allah preserve us from misfortune and madness!" or "May Allah bring him back to light and life!" In this way he cultivated the power of being invisible.

Nobody understood the meaning of his retreat. His

mother, who might have understood, was too concerned with her own sick body and her tottering reason. He spent his time shaving and removing the hairs from his legs. He was hoping for some radical change in the destiny that had been more or less given him. For that he needed time, a lot of time, just as he needed some stranger's eye to light on his changing body as it returned to its origins, as nature resumed her rights. Despite some irritation, he continued to correspond with that anonymous friend. Allow me, my dear companions, to open the book once again and read to you:

Tuesday, April 13. Never again, my friend, will I touch on the problems concerning your family. If I have lacked discretion, it was because of the excess of feeling that tormented and disturbed me. Why did I embark on this correspondence, in which each sentence exchanged merely complicates our labyrinth, in which we grope our way, our eyes blindfolded, at the risk of never meeting?

I am and always have been a creature of intuition. When I found myself on your tracks, I was guided by that strong, indefinable feeling. I have observed you from afar and was touched—physically—by the waves that you emitted. Perhaps you do not believe in this kind of communication, but I knew at once that I was dealing with an exceptional individual, one existing outside his own being, outside his body. I felt, in the physical sense, that you were not a man like others. My curiosity became a passion. My intuition oppressed me, drove me ever deeper into my search, bringing me ever closer to you. I have written many letters that I have not sent you. Each time I hesitated and wondered by what right I was pursuing you with my questions and why I was so determined to give back to your face its original image and features.

How could I have confronted you otherwise? What I had to say to you is not said in our society, especially not in public. I am impatient to know your feelings on what I have just confessed to you. Our correspondence has now reached a threshold of complicity that commits us to each other and puts our future at stake.

To conclude, I would like to whisper to you at dawn these lines by the mystical poet of the thirteenth century, Ibn Al-Fârid:

> *And if night surrounds you and buries these homes in*
>   *their solitude,*
> *light a fire in their darkness with desire.* . . .
>   Yours.

9

"Construct a face as one constructs a house"

Before going on with my reading of this journal, I would like, for those who are concerned about the fate of the rest of the family, to mention that after the death of the unfortunate Fatima our character lost his grip on his business and shut himself up, never to appear in public again. He was suspected of bringing about his wife's death, and the two families became enemies forever.

Things gradually got worse. Cracks appeared in the walls of the big house, and the trees in the courtyard died of neglect. The mother felt this decline as vengeance from heaven for diverting God's will. She sank into a gentle, silent madness. The daughters who had remained at home squandered the money of the inheritance and tried, in one way or another, to harm their hidden brother. But that brother was out of reach: invisible, he continued to reign in spite of everything. At night his footsteps could be heard, but nobody saw him. Doors and windows were closed on an oppressive mystery. He had got into the habit of hanging on his door a schoolboy's slate, on which he wrote in white chalk some thought—a word, a verse from the Koran, a prayer. Who was this intended for? Malika could not read. His sisters never dared go up to his room. But almost every day had its own thought, its own color, its own music.

On the day now reached by our story, one could read on the slate, "What does the night say? Go home!"

Another day there was this verse: "We belong to God and we shall return to him." And he had added, in small characters, "if I wish." Heresy! Heresy! Brothers! From that stage on, his solitude became broader and deeper, until it became his sole purpose and companion. Every now and then he was tempted to abandon it, to go out and, in an access of madness and destructive fury, overturn everything. I'm not sure that one will see what is going to happen, even reading his journal and correspondence.

April 15. I have put myself through enough. Now I am trying to spare myself. For me it was a wager. I almost lost it. To be a woman is a natural infirmity and every woman gets used to it. To be a man is an illusion, an act of violence that requires no justification. Simply to be is a challenge. I am tired. Were it not for this body to be mended, this worn piece of material to be patched, this voice already low and husky, this weak chest and this wounded look, if there were not those narrow-minded souls, that sacred book, those words spoken in the cave, and that spite that bars the way to intruders and protects, if there were not the asthma that tires the heart and the kief that takes me far away from this room, if there were not this deep sadness pursuing me—I would open these windows and scale the highest walls to reach the crests of solitude, my only hope, my refuge, my mirror, and the path of my dreams.

April 16. Someone said that "voices echo differently in solitude"! How does one speak in an empty, isolated glass cage? In a low voice, an inner voice, so low and deep that it becomes an echo of a thought yet unformulated.

I am apprenticing myself to silence, which withdraws from time to time, giving place to the echo of my secret thoughts; these surprise me with their strangeness.

April 16, evening. I fell asleep in my bath. I love the steam from the water, the mist that covers the windows of my cage. My thoughts play, become diluted in that evaporated water and begin to dance like tiny circus sparks. The dreams one has in that state of abandonment are sweet and dangerous. A man came, crossing the mist and the space, and laid his hand on my damp face. My eyes closed, I let him continue as I lay in the already tepid water. He put his heavy hand on my breast, which awoke, plunged his head into the water, and placed it on my stomach, kissing my sex. What I then felt was so strong that I lost consciousness and almost drowned. I woke as the water was entering my half-open mouth.

I was shaken throughout my whole being. I got out of the bath, dried myself, and went back to my bed, my books, and my obsessions.

April 17, morning. I am still suffering from the shock of yesterday's dream. Was it a dream? Did he really come? My capacity for resistance is immeasurable. I have lost my

71

body's language; indeed, I never possessed it. I ought to learn it, starting out by speaking as a woman. Why as a woman? Am I a man? This will require a journey. I shall have to retrace my steps patiently, rediscover the earliest sensations of a body that neither head nor reason controls. How am I to speak, and to whom?

That reminds me—I have received no letter from my correspondent. He is too serious. Shall I have the nerve to show myself to him one day? I must answer his last letter. I don't want to write. I'll let a few days go by. We'll see if he makes an appearance. It was he who visited me in my bath. I recognized his voice, an inner voice, the voice that comes through his writing; it slants, like the words he crosses out. When I reread certain of his letters, a shiver runs through my whole body. It is as if his sentences were stroking my skin, touching me at the most sensitive points of my body. Ah! I need serenity to awaken this body; there is still time to bring it back to the desire that belongs to it.

. . . What does my conscience say? . . . My conscience has said nothing all this time. . . . It was elsewhere, asleep, like dough made with bad yeast. . . . It might breathe into my mouth, as if to revive a drowned woman, the words "You must become who you are. . . ." It might arise. . . . But it lies beneath thick layers of clay, and the clay stops me from breathing. . . . It's funny—tomorrow I could appear before a judge and proudly tell him that I am lodging a complaint against the clay that lies upon my conscience, stifling it, preventing me from becoming what I am! I can just see the round, astonished head of the judge, no more corrupt than any other, though I shall choose one who breathes corruption as naturally as air. . . . Judges are not noted for their humor and tend not to make one laugh. . . . If I went out dressed as a man, I would follow the judge and corner him in some dark entrance and kiss him on the mouth. . . . They disgust me, all these images. . . . My lips are so pure they'll curl back the day they are laid on other lips. . . . Anyway, why should they be placed on other lips? . . . Yet, in my dreams, I see only fleshy lips passing over my body and pausing for a long time on my sex. . . . It gives me such pleasure that I wake up . . . and find my own hand there. . . . That's enough of that. . . . What does my conscience say? Open one of the windows and look straight at the sun. . . .

April 19. A miserable day. I open the window. The sky has cleared. I'm learning to look at myself in the mirror. I'm learning to see my body, first dressed, then naked. I'm rather thin. My breasts are so small. Only my buttocks have anything feminine about them. I've decided to remove the hairs from my legs and find the words for the return. I have almost acquired the rhythm and bearing of that return. It will be day inverted into a starless night. I shall weave the nights together and no longer see day, with its light, its colors, and its mysteries.

For some time I have felt liberated, yes, ready to be a woman. But I am told, I tell myself, that before that I must go back to childhood, become a little girl, an adolescent girl, a girl in love, a woman. . . . What a long path. I shall never get there.

April 20. I have now put myself on probation. I feel like the philosopher's camel, which had difficult tastes and desires that were impossible to satisfy and which said:

If I were allowed to choose freely,
I would choose a little place
In the middle of Paradise:
Better still—before its gate!

April 20, night. Project for a letter. Friend, you are becoming demanding, insistent, worried. I'm in the middle of a mutation. I am going from myself to myself, limping a bit, hesitating, dragging my feet like an invalid. I am on my way, but I don't know when or where this journey will end. Your letter disturbed me. You know a great deal about me, and when I read your letters I see my garments fall one after another to the ground. How have you been able to penetrate the cage of secrecy? Do you think your emotions will be capable of teaching me to live once more? To breathe without thinking I'm breathing, to walk without thinking I'm walking, to put my hands on someone else's skin without hesitation, and to laugh at nothing in particular, like a child moved by a sunbeam?

How can I answer you when I haven't yet found myself, experiencing only the inverted emotions that come from a betrayed body reduced to an empty, soulless home?

I have voluntarily cut myself off from the rest of the world. I have excluded myself from my family, from society, and from this body that I have inhabited for so long. You speak to me of your physical disturbances. Isn't this anticipation? My pleasure lies in guessing what you are like, drawing the features of your face, re-creating your body out of your sentences. I know your voice already: it is low, slightly husky, warm when you let yourself go. . . . Tell me if I'm mistaken. Have you never tried to become the voice of the absent one, a philosopher, a poet,

74

a prophet? I believe I know the voice of our Prophet Mohammed. I know that he did not speak much; he had a
calm, steady, pure voice; nothing troubled it. I refer to the
voice because mine has undergone such a transformation.
I hear myself shouting deep down within myself. Each cry
is a descent into myself—a descent, not a fall. It's almost
a euphoria. To be able to shout and hear oneself . . . To
glide gently into oneself, into this carcass . . . When I read
a book, I amuse myself by listening to the author's voice.
What is odd is that I often confuse the voice of a man with
that of a woman, a child's with that of an adult. Sometimes
your voice reaches me wrapped in something feminine—
in fact, everything depends on the moment when I read
your letters. When I'm angry and my eyes land on one
of them, it is the soft, unbearable voice of a woman
that I hear. Who are you? Never tell me! Until the next
time.

P.S. From now on, leave your letters at the jeweler's,
which is just opposite my shop. I no longer trust my staff.
Better to be prudent!

Have you noticed that the sky has just taken on a strange
mauve color? It's the full moon. Every kind of madness
is permitted. . . .

April 22. I forgot to give the letter to Malika to take
to the jeweler's. I forget a lot of things these days. The
darkness helps me to think, and when my thoughts wander
I still cling to the darkness, as if someone were throwing
me a rope, which I take and swing on until I have re-
established calm in my home. I need all my energy to
concentrate on a question that I have so far avoided. I dare
not speak of it yet, even to myself.

75

There are silences that are like stifled sobbings in the night.

I haven't seen the naked body of a woman or a man since the time when I used to go to the hammam as a child. Bodies come and inhabit certain of my dreams; they touch me, stroke me, and go away. Everything takes place in the secrets of sleep. When I wake, I feel as though something has gone through me and left slight scratches on its way, as if my skin had been clawed, but without pain, without violence. I can never distinguish between the faces. The body of a man, or of a woman? My head retains only confused images. When I had a life in the outside world, when I went out and traveled, I noticed how hungry people are for sex. When the men look at a woman they petrify her body; each look tears off her jellaba and dress. They weigh her buttocks and breasts and feel their virile members inside their gandouras.

Occasionally I caught a glimpse of my father, dressed but with his trousers down, giving my mother the white seed; he was bent over her, saying nothing; she was hardly moving. I was very small. I retained that image, which I was to rediscover with the animals on our farm. I was very young, but not taken in. I knew what the whitish seed was—I had already seen it in the men's hammam. I was young and it disgusted me. Having caught sight of that ridiculous, comic scene, I was inconsolable. I ran off to forget that image and bury it in the earth, under a pile of stones. But it came back, enlarged, transformed, moving. My father was in a more and more ridiculous position, gesticulating, swinging his loose buttocks; my mother entwining her agile legs around his back, yelling; he hit her to keep her quiet and she shouted still louder, laughing at him. Those entwined bodies were grotesque. Still very

76

young, I was sitting on the edge of the bed, so small they couldn't see me, but receptive, stuck there. The bed moved and squeaked; my eyes were larger than my face; my nose captured all the smells; I was suffocating; I was coughing and nobody heard me. I tried to pull myself free, to get up and run off to vomit and spit. But though I pulled and pulled, I couldn't move. I pulled at myself even harder, until I wrenched myself free, leaving the skin of my buttocks on the wooden floor. My backside bleeding, I ran, crying, into a wood just outside the town. I was so small, and it seemed as if my father's huge member was pursuing me, as if it caught me and brought me back home. . . . I could breathe at last, breathe again. . . . All those images are now far away. . . .

My head is heavy. Where can I lay it? Put it away in a round cardboard box on a shelf with the hats. Lay it out delicately on midnight-blue velvet. Cover it with a silk scarf. Put in a roll of cotton or a piece of wood to keep it from moving. Pass my hand over the eyes to close them. Carefully comb the hair—don't pull on it. Calmly. Don't get excited. Walk barefoot. Be careful not to wake the objects, a broken clock, a one-eyed porcelain dog, a wooden spoon, a sorry-looking armchair, a worn low table, a black stone for ablutions in the desert, this bed, these sheets, that chair near the closed window (it's the chair of nostalgia), that prayer mat. I would like to lose my head, if only for once. My body turned in upon itself, I would wait for my head to be brought back in a bunch of roses soaked in jasmine water. Ah! If I had to be separated from everything that stops me from breathing and sleeping, very little would be left. I would be nothing—a thought. . . .

It is no longer I who crosses the night. It is it that drags me down into its limbo. . . .

April 25. On my breakfast tray is a sheet of paper folded in four. A sign from my distant friend:

"Isn't resembling oneself the same as becoming different?" I go away for a time. I move away from you and come closer to myself. I am reduced to absolute solitude. An alien within my own family, I am negligible, absolutely negligible. Odd and isolated. You know my passions: reading certain mystical poets and dogging your steps. I teach students the love of the absolute. Poor me! I shall write to you at greater length soon. I send you the light of this spring.

The same morning. I don't know whether it is good fortune or a trap to be able to go away, to travel, to wander, to forget. Ever since I took to this room, I go out and see the city through your eyes and with your words. I need to travel, far from here. You know very well that my homeland is not a country, still less a family. It is a look, a face, an encounter, a long night of silence and tenderness. I shall stay here, motionless, awaiting your letters; reading them is like going away. I shall be a locker in which you keep your log book, page by page. I shall keep those pages out of friendship, out of love. I shall write to you and hand everything back to you on your return. We shall exchange our syllables until our hands may touch. . . .

I thank you for the light of the spring. Friend, here I see neither light nor spring, but myself against myself in the eternal return of an impossible passion.

Have a good journey! And if you meet a child with moist eyes,

Know that it is a little of my past that is kissing you.

May. I have lost all notion of time. Curiously enough, my calendar stopped at the end of April. There are some pages missing. Some hand has torn them out. My time is nothing like that of the calendar, whether complete or not.

This morning I thought of adopting a child. A short-lived idea that was dropped as quickly as it came into my head. A child? I could have one with anybody, the milk-man, the muezzin, the man who washes the dead—anybody, provided he were blind. Why not abduct some handsome youth, blindfold him, and reward him with a night in which he will not see my face but may do whatever he likes with my body? This would require accomplices, and I have no wish to run the risk of exposure. But my body has had increasingly specific desires recently, and I don't know what to do to satisfy them. Another, odd idea: to live with a cat! At least she will not know who I am; for her I would be a human, sexless presence.

I have learned that my sisters have left the house. They went away one by one; my mother has shut herself up in one of the rooms and, in accordance with her wishes, is purging a century of silence and confinement. The house is enormous. It is in a poor state of repair; in fact, it is falling to pieces. I keep to one end, my mother to the other. She knows where I am, but I don't know where she is. Malika serves us both and helps us, each in her own particular ordeal.

Is it night in the night or still day in the night? Something trembles within me. It must be my soul.

10

*The Storyteller Devoured
by His Words*

Faithful companions! Not many of you have followed me
through this man's story, but the number is not important.
I know why some did not come back this morning: they
could not bear the minor heresy that our character allowed
himself. He dared to distort a line from the Koran. But he
is a creature who no longer belongs to himself. He has
been diverted from his destiny, and if, at the moment when
he undergoes a crisis, he takes some liberty with a line, a
single line, we should be able to forgive him. Besides, we
are not his judges. God will take care of that.

Something or someone is holding us back, in any case;
a heavy, serene hand binds us together, obtaining for us
the light of patience. The morning wind brings health to
the sick and opens the gates to the faithful. At that moment,
the wind turns the pages of the book and awakens the
syllables one by one; sentences or lines arise and dissipate
the mist of expectation. I love that wind, which envelops
us and draws the sleep from our eyes. It upsets the order

of the text and scatters the insects that have become stuck to the thick pages.

I see a moth escape from the handwritten words. It carries off with it a few useless images. I see a swallow trying to free itself from a jumble of words smeared with rare oil. I see a bat beating its wings in the distance of the book. It heralds the end of a season, perhaps the end of an era. The wind leafing through the book intoxicates me; it takes me up to the top of a hill, where I sit down on a stone and look down at the city. Everybody seems to be asleep, as if the entire city were nothing but an enormous cemetery. And I, in this inaccessible place, am alone with the book and its inhabitants. I hear the murmur of water; it may be a stream that has found its way into the pages of the book, skipping through the chapters. The water doesn't wash away all the sentences; is this because the ink resists, or because the water chooses its passages? How strange! I have often dreamed of a hand passing over the pages of an already written book, cleaning it inside, removing whatever was useless and pompous, hollow and superfluous.

Fragmentary, but not without meaning, the event is stamped on my consciousness. The manuscript I wanted to read to you falls to pieces whenever I try to open it and free its words, which poison so many birds, insects, and images. Fragmentary, it possesses me, obsesses me, and brings me back to you, you who have the patience to wait. The book is like a house in which each window is a district, each door a town, each page a street; it is only a sham house, a theatrical set in which the moon and sky are represented by a lightbulb and a blue sheet held between two windows.

We are going to live in this big house. In it the sun rises early and dawn is tumultuous. That is as it should be—it is the hour of writing, the moment when the rooms and walls, the streets and floors move—or, rather, are moved by the profusion of words. It is the hour of feverish movement, sudden comings and goings, and descents. It is a solemn hour, when everyone withdraws to meditate and to record the signs struck by the syllables. The house keeps its serene façade, aloof from all this bustle inside. We shall be inside the walls, in the courtyard, in the square from which fan out as many streets as nights. The stories of those nights will have to be told if we are not to be engulfed by them. In any case, they must not be allowed to flow together before the break of day! We shall have a few moments' respite to recover our breath and remember.

We are now alone together. Our character is about to get up. We catch a glimpse of him, but he does not see us. He thinks he is alone. He does not feel spied upon. All the better. Let us listen to his steps, follow his breathing, draw the veil from his tired soul. He has no news of his anonymous correspondent.

11

The Man with a Woman's Breasts

My retirement has lasted long enough. I must have gone beyond the limits that I imposed upon myself. Who am I now? I dare not look at myself in the mirror. What is the state of my skin, my façade, my appearance? Too much solitude and silence have exhausted me. I have surrounded myself with books and secrecy. Today I am trying to deliver myself. From what, exactly? From the fear that I have piled up? From that layer of mist that served me as a veil? From that relationship with the other in myself, he who writes to me and gives me the strange impression of being in this world? To deliver myself from destiny, or from the witnesses of my early years? The idea of death is too familiar to me to provide a refuge, so I shall go out. It is time to be born again. I am not actually going to change, but will simply return to myself—just before the destiny that was laid down for me begins to unroll and carries me off on its current.

To go out. To emerge from underground. My body

would raise the heavy stones from that destiny and stand like a new thing on the ground. Ah! The idea of subtracting myself from that memory brings me joy. I had forgotten what joy is! What relief, what pleasure in thinking that it would be my own hands that would mark out the route of a street that might lead to a mountain! It has taken me a long time to reach this window. I feel light. Am I about to shout out with joy or to sing? I shall go away and leave this unmade life. My life is like this bed and these sheets rumpled by lassitude, by the long nights, by the solitude imposed on this body. I am going to leave without putting my affairs in order, without any luggage, just money and this manuscript, the unique trace and witness of what was my calvary. It is half blackened with ink. I hope to write happier stories in the other half. I shall stop the deathly beasts from slipping into it and leave the pages open to butterflies and certain wild roses. They will sleep on a softer bed, where the words will no longer be pebbles, but fig leaves. They will dry with time, without losing either their color or their scents.

I have taken off the bandages around my chest. I have stroked my sex at length. It didn't give me pleasure—or, rather, I had violent sensations, like electrical shocks. I knew that the return to myself would take time, that I had to re-educate my emotions and reject old habits. My retirement was not enough; that is why I decided to make this body face adventure, on the roads, in other towns, in other places.

My first encounter was a misunderstanding. An old beggarwoman or witch, a cunning vagabond, wrapped in multicolored rags, a disturbing look in her bright eyes, crossed my path in one of those narrow alleyways, so dark and narrow that it was nicknamed Zankat Wahed, the Street of a Single Man. She barred my way. It wasn't difficult: one had only to stand in the middle and raise one's arms a little to reach the walls. She blocked the light and kept the air from passing. Thus, in its first steps without a mask, my body, which wanted to be anonymous and ordinary beneath its jellaba, confronted its morning ordeal in the person of an old witch with a lined, rocklike face.

"Who are you?" she asked sharply.

I was ready to answer any question, to invent, to imagine innumerable replies, but that question alone threw me into confusion and literally struck me dumb. I was not about to enter into a detailed account of what my life had been. In any case, the old woman suspected something. There was not a trace of innocence in her eyes. She was scrutinizing me, undressing me, putting me to the test; she knew something and was seeking confirmation, impatiently. The question came back with the same domineering tone:

"What are you hiding under your jellaba, a man or a woman, a child or an old man, a dove or a spider? Answer or you will not leave this street. Anyway, it isn't a street, but a dead end. I hold the keys to it and I filter the air and light that traverse it."

"You know very well who I am, so let me pass."

"What I know matters little to you! But I want to hear you yourself tell me who you really are. I don't want a name. I desire the invisible, what you are hiding, what you are holding prisoner in your rib cage."

"I myself don't know. I have only just emerged from a long labyrinth in which each question was a burn. My body is plowed with wounds and scars, and yet it is a body that has lived little. I have only just emerged from the shadows. . . ."

"The shadows or darkness?"

"Solitude, silence, the terrible mirror."

"You mean passion. . . ."

"Alas, yes! Passion for oneself in thick, heavy solitude."

"So, since you cannot name that body, show it."

Since I hesitated, she threw herself on me and, with her strong hands, tore off my jellaba, then my shift. When she saw my two small breasts, her face became gentle, illuminated by a disturbing light in which desire mingled with surprise. She gently moved her hands over my chest, then put her lips to the nipple of my right breast, kissed it, sucked it. Her mouth was toothless; it had the softness of a baby's lips. At first I did not stop her; then I reacted violently, pushing her aside with all my strength. She fell over and I took to my heels, trying to close up my jellaba.

This encounter had no consequences, at least not immediately. However, what happened afterward disturbed me a great deal. Must I speak of it? I find it difficult to write about it. I mean, I'm ashamed of it. I can feel my cheeks redden at the mere thought of that day, when everything in my mind was turned upside down and my emotion churned up. The physical sensation I felt as that toothless mouth caressed my breast was pleasurable, even if it lasted only a few seconds. I am ashamed to admit it.

That night I slept in a luxurious hotel room, trying to forget. But I was pursued by the image of that almost black face, smiling at me as if to remind me of a memory from another life. The woman had a limp, which I hadn't noticed. Her voice was not entirely strange to me; it was part of my childhood. Then, all night, I could not get the face of my mad, amnesiac mother out of my mind. It gradually replaced that of the old woman and made me feel ill. I had booked into the hotel under my official identity, but I noticed the worried look of the porter. My sentences remained unfinished. I lay down on the bed naked and tried to revive the pleasure that had been forbidden my senses. For a long time I stroked my breasts and the lips of my vagina. I was overcome with emotion. I was ashamed. The discovery of my body was to pass through that encounter between my hands and my vagina. Gently my fingers brushed over my skin. I was in a sweat, I was trembling, and I still don't know whether what I felt was pleasure or disgust. I washed, then sat down in front of the mirror and looked at that body. A mist formed on the glass, and I could hardly see myself. I liked that vague, unstable image; it corresponded to the state in which my soul was bathed. I shaved my armpits, perfumed myself, and returned to bed, as if I were seeking some forgotten sensation or liberating emotion—to free myself.

These caresses in front of the mirror became a habit, a sort of pact between my body and its image, an image buried long ago that had to be awoken as my fingers lightly touched my skin. I would write before or after these sessions. I often lacked inspiration, because I discovered that the caresses accompanied by images were more intense. I did not know where to get them. I would invent a few, but it was no use; they wouldn't work, just as I sometimes spent hours in front of the white page. My body was that page and that book. In order to awaken, it had to be fed, wrapped in images, filled with syllables and emotions, maintained in the sweetness of things, and given dreams.

I found myself once again locked away. I could not forget my first encounter, but I could not give up or go back on my decision at any cost. To break with my family was natural, necessary, useful. The break with myself was of a different order, not even one that I had imposed upon myself. In fact, I was improvising—forestalling, at the whim of chance, a destiny whose violence I scarcely suspected.

I no longer recall what town I was in. I remember the sea and the ancient walls, fishermen's boats painted in blue and pink, ships eroded by rust and time, an island with rare birds, a forbidden island, a Marabout tomb on the edge of the town, haunted by sterile women, white streets, cracked walls, an old Jew dozing on the terrace of a big café, one of the last Jews in the medina, badly dressed tourists, clever street urchins, the cemetery by the sea, tables set up on the quayside at which people were eating grilled sardines. Two men were mending a fishing net, sitting on the ground, legs crossed, talking. I remember some of their words:

"That's time. . . ."

"Time and those who are masters of it . . ."

"The women . . ."

"They aren't women any more; they go out, they're indoors, eyes open, wearing tight belts. . . ."

"This net will be worthless. . . ."

"And the men?"

I've forgotten what the other man replied. Perhaps nothing. A silence filled by the wind and waves.

It was no doubt in that town governed by night and mists that I met Um Abbas. She came to fetch me as if she had been sent by someone. Night had just fallen, and it was very warm. I felt her hand on my shoulder as I was sitting on the terrace of the only café in the town.

"One of the Prophet's companions has sent me after you," she said. "I've been looking for you for a long time. Say nothing. Let me guess what you are going to say."

Terrified, I actually preferred silence. She drew up a chair and sat down next to me. I was overcome by a smell of cloves—a horrible smell, especially when mixed with sweat. She leaned forward and said: "I know you."

I tried to move away a little, but her hand gripped me and held me prisoner. Could I shout out? No. Call for help? What was the point? She let go of my arm and said firmly, "You will follow me!"

I did not even pretend to resist. Could I escape that call? Was it possible to circumvent destiny? Besides, how else did I expect an adventure would begin?

What was that old messenger like? What image should I attribute to her face? Kindness, cunning, cruelty? Let's say she had prominent front teeth, which overhung her bruised lower lip; her forehead was shallow, heavily furrowed; her cheeks hollow; but her eyes shone with a bright intelligence.

I had decided to go along with her and let things happen to me. I followed her in silence. When we reached a dark alleyway, she cornered me against a wall and started to search me. I soon realized that she was looking neither for money nor for jewelry. Her hands roamed over my body as if to verify an intuition. My tiny breasts did not reassure her; she slipped her hand into my trousers and left it for a moment on my sex, then inserted her middle finger. It hurt. I uttered a cry, which she stifled by putting her other hand over my mouth, saying, "I wasn't sure."

"Nor was I!" I said between my teeth. A circus had

been set up on the edge of the town, near a huge square where storytellers and snake charmers performed year in and year out to a large, faithful public.

A thick crowd had gathered in front of the booth where a showman was urging people to buy lottery tickets; he was yelling into a hand-held microphone mechanical formulas in an Arabic mixed with a few words of French, Spanish, English, and even some imaginary language of his own, the language of circus people familiar with all manner of swindling:

"Errrrbeh . . . Errrrbeh . . . One million . . . Mellioune . . . Talvaza bilaluan . . . One color television . . . A Mercedes . . . Errrrbeh! One thousand . . . Three thousand . . . Arba Alaf . . . Turn, turn the wheel of fortune. . . . Aiua! Krista . . . Amourrrre . . . All that's left, baqali Achr'a billetat . . . Achr'a . . . Aiua . . . Again . . . L'aventurrrre . . . The wheel will turn. . . . But before . . . before you are going to see and hear. . . . Tferju we tsatabu raskum fe, the beautiful Malika . . . She sings and dances Farid El Atrash!! Malika!"

From behind the shelves on which the various prizes were displayed emerged Malika. She had a beard of several days' growth and a magnificent mustache that fell over badly made-up lips. Malika was wearing an old-fashioned caftan and a belt embroidered with gold thread. It was obvious that her breasts consisted of rags, which kept slipping out of place. She danced to the music of Farid El Atrash. If you got closer, you could see the hairs on her legs. She grabbed the microphone from the master of ceremonies and performed a few steps, swinging her hips. The crowd was suitably impressed, and yet nobody was taken in. Malika was obviously a man. There was something strange and at the same time familiar about him. Complicity brought the crowd together in good humor and laughter. The man danced a woman's dance, miming to Farid El Atrash, exciting the men in the crowd, winking at some, blowing kisses to others. . . .

I had already heard of those circus shows in which men dress up as female dancers without really passing themselves off as women, in which there is an atmosphere of derision, without any real ambiguity. There was even a famous actor possessed of a particularly masculine voice and appearance who specialized in playing women's roles, usually shrews who dominated men and made them ridiculous. He was called Bu Shayb and was utterly lacking in feminine charm. When he died, his eldest son tried to take over his roles, but without success.

Abbas, the old woman's son, came toward me and made a sign for me to follow him. Malika was no longer dancing, but readjusting her bust, in full view of the audience. She had a cigarette in the corner of her mouth and had closed one eye against the smoke. Abbas was the master of ceremonies and boss of the show. When he spoke to me, he no longer rolled his "r"s:

"We are nomads; there's something exciting about our life, but it isn't an easy one. Everything is false, and that's what we're about. We don't hide it. People come for that, for Malika, who is no more a dancing girl out of the thousand and one nights than I'm the man in the moon. They come for the lottery. The wheel of fortune is rigged, of course. They suspect as much, but accept it all the same. Only the donkey that smokes and pretends to be dead is real—it's a donkey I've trained and it costs me dear because I feed it well. The young acrobats are all orphans, and I'm their father and brother. When they get on my nerves, I beat them. That's how it is. In this country, you put others down or they put you down. So I rule with a heavy hand. Take it or leave it. My mother isn't a witch, despite appearances to the contrary. She's a saint. She runs the business, reads the cards, and finds the artists. She brought me Malika, but the fool is leaving us. His wife has threatened to leave him. He's leaving, and you're going to replace him. We'll change the style of the number: you'll dress up as a man in the first part of the show; then you'll disappear for five minutes and reappear as a *femme fatale*. . . . There's enough there to drive all the men in the audience wild. It'll be very exciting. I can see it now—a real show, with proper staging, suspense, and even a bit of nudity, not much, just a leg, a thigh. . . . It's a shame your breasts aren't very big: the men around here love big breasts and buttocks. You're too thin, but it doesn't matter. We'll have to work on the gestures and innuendoes! You'll begin tomorrow. Sometimes men get excited and throw bank notes at the dancer. You'll pick them up and give them to me. No fooling around!"

I said nothing throughout this long speech. I was fascinated. Slowly, but jerkily, I was beginning to realize what kind of person I should become. I shuddered. Was that the emotion of a body summoned by another life, new adventures?

I slept in a tent. Around me I recognized the young acrobats, who were very discreet. They gave off a smell of straw and urine, so intense it nearly knocked me out. The night was long and heavy. I had dream after dream. Horses' heads baked to a cinder in the sand. An open hand eaten by red ants. Song after song, lacking all melody and harmony. A man with a shaven head and one leg was whipping a tree. A street rose and rose until it became lost in the twilit sky. The young acrobats climbed one on top of another and formed a pyramid. They were not doing a turn, but helping an old asthmatic to get to heaven; they thought they would be able to lay him at the threshold of paradise. The pyramid was very high. I couldn't see the top, which was lost in a cloud. The sick man's tiny body was passed from hand to hand. He was happy; this was the way he wanted to go. He didn't want his soul to get to heaven without him. The boys were laughing. The boss was organizing the operation with his hand-held microphone. It was a gentle death, like that of birds dropping out of the sky. The old man was holding a handkerchief and waving us a last goodbye with it. He was light and smiled a lot. Then there was silence. The boss disappeared. The boys came down one after another, holding the old man's clothes. Mission accomplished. Last time they had sent the boss's grandfather to heaven in this way. They said it was very mild up there. They laid the old man on a fairly thick layer of cloud and waited for other hands to take him. They weren't allowed to say any more; besides, they didn't know anything. They were quite content to form the ladder and provide the transport. The rest was not their business.

That first night was interminable. The suffocating smell of the horses urinating on the straw must have caused me to have those visions, of which I could remember only the most striking. Next day I remembered a man's face, made up like a woman's. The man was crying, and his tears made the makeup run down over his beard and mustache. He was crying for no reason and wanted me to give him my breast, as if he were an infant who had been weaned too early. When he came up to me, I recognized the old woman who had brought me into this situation; she had disguised herself as Malika and was really crying.

In the morning I made a few attempts to perform on the boards. The old woman stuck on my lips the mustache that she herself had worn in my dream and powdered my cheeks with some black substance by way of a beard. The caftan was very old and dirty. It was still impregnated with numerous applications of cheap perfume. She called me Zahra, "Amirat Lhob," "Princess of Love." I performed to order; my curiosity was driving me to go further. I might not know anything about this "family of artistes," but I did hope to know more about myself.

I had no fears. On the contrary, I was jubilant, radiant, as if a weight had been lifted from my shoulders.

12

The Woman with the Badly Shaven Beard

At the back, not of the stage, but of this story, hangs a wide, multicolored ribbon; swollen by the wind, it becomes a transparent bird that dances on the farthest point of the horizon, as if to give this adventure the colors and melodies it needs. When the wind is only a summer breeze, the ribbon floats to the regular rhythm of a horse galloping to infinity; on the horse is a rider wearing a large hat on which some unknown hand has laid ears of corn, branches of bay, and wild flowers. When he stops over there, at the point when day is indistinguishable from night, on those lands where the stones have been painted by children, where the walls serve as beds to statues, there, in immobility and silence, under the gaze of loving girls, he becomes a tree that stands awake all night. In the morning, the first rays of light surround the tree, move it, give it body and memories, then freeze it in the marble of a statue with arms laden with foliage and fruit. All around is a white, bare space in which everything melts on arrival, turning to sand, crystal, and small, chiseled stones. Opposite the statue of the morning is a large old mirror; it reflects not the statue but the tree, for it is an object with a memory. The clock is a soulless mechanism; it has stopped, worn by rust and use, by time, by men's breathing.

Friends! Time is the curtain that will soon fall on the spectacle and envelop our character under a shroud.

Companions! The stage is made of paper! The story that I am telling you is an old piece of wrapping paper. It will need only a match, a torch, to confine everything to nothingness. The same fire would burn down the gates and the days. Only our character would escape! He alone would be capable of finding a refuge and the rest of our story amid the pile of ashes.

In his book he speaks of an island. It may be his new home, the hinterland, the hinter-story, the last stretch, the infinite whiteness of silence.

Our character—I don't know what to call him or her—became the main attraction of the circus. He drew men and women and brought a great deal of money to the owner. He was far from his native city, and his disappearance had little impact on the big, dilapidated house. He danced and sang. His body found the joy and happiness of a youth in love. She hid herself to write. The old woman watched over her. Abbas protected her. Sometimes a man, sometimes a woman, our character was moving toward the reconquest of his being. He no longer slept with the acrobats, but in the women's tent; she ate and went out with the other women. She was called Lalla Zahra, a name she became fond of. She indulged in no nostalgia; she rejected the flood of memories. The break with the past was not easy. Then she invented those white spaces, where with one hand she launched crazy images and with the other dressed them with a taste for life, the life of which she dreamed.

She aspired to calm and serenity—especially to write. One night, as she was going back onstage, she found a letter lying on her straw bed:

Lalla, so the evidence is a window misted over. Even the sun—the light that dazzles you in the evening—yearns for shade.

Just when I had to leave and even to disappear, it was you who took the road of exile. Since the day I recognized you, I have been in the audience every evening. I look at you, observe you, and distance myself. I would not want to embarrass you or importune you with the intensity of my emotions. Know that I am not following you in order to spy on you; I am following you in order to have the illusion of acceding to the inaccessible.

Humbly, faithfully yours.

You may write to me and leave me a letter at the cash desk, bearing the words Al Majhul. It will never be I who comes to collect it, but someone else.

Good night.

She was overcome with emotion. It was a long time since the Anonymous One had manifested himself. On the other side of the room, the old woman pretended to be asleep. An ashtray and a glass of water containing the old woman's false teeth stood on a stool. Lalla Zahra was sitting on the bed, deep in thought. A groping hand slipped into the glass and seized the teeth. The old woman wanted to know what was going on:

"Who has written to you?"

"Nobody!"

"And that letter?"

"I don't know where it has come from or who wrote it."

"Be careful! We don't want any trouble. If an admirer turns up, I know how to get rid of him."

"Yes, that's it! It must be some madman chasing me. Yet I know nobody here."

"It's quite simple. If it's a man, you're a man; if it's a woman, I'll take care of her!"

She pulled out her false teeth and put them back in the glass. Lalla shut her eyes and tried to sleep.

Docile and submissive, Lalla Zahra thus underwent a long season of purgation in order to forget. She never disobeyed the old woman and carefully kept her thoughts for the night. She wrote in secret, while others were asleep, writing everything down on school exercise books. Though she managed to distance her past from herself, she could not efface it. A few strong, cruel images remained imprinted in her mind: the authoritarian father, the mad mother, the epileptic wife.

13

A Night without Escape

I sense them there behind me, pursuing me with their mocking laughter, throwing stones at me. I see first my father, young and strong, advancing toward me, dagger in hand, determined to cut my throat or to tie me up and bury me alive. I hear his rough, terrifying voice coming back from far away, calmly and quietly, to put some order back into this story. He speaks of betrayal and justice. When I hear him, I no longer see him. His image disappears and hides behind the walls, and it is objects that speak: the nearest tree, or even the tottering statue placed as if by mistake in the middle of a crossroads. The voice comes nearer; it makes the glasses on the table vibrate; it is the wind that carries it and holds me prisoner. I cannot escape it; I am there and I listen to it:

"Before Islam, Arab fathers threw an unwanted female infant into a hole and covered her until she died. They were right. In this way they rid themselves of misfortune. It was an act of wisdom, a brief pain, an implacable logic.

I have always been fascinated by the courage of those fathers—a courage I never had. All the daughters your mother gave birth to deserved such a fate. I did not bury them, because they did not exist for me. You were different; you were a challenge. But you betrayed me. I shall pursue you until your dying day. You will find no peace. Sooner or later the damp earth will fall on your face, enter your gaping mouth, your nostrils, your lungs. You will return to earth and it will be as if you never existed. I shall come back and with my hand pile earth upon your body. . . . Ahmed, my son, the man I formed, is dead. You, woman, are merely a usurper. You are stealing that man's life; you will die for the theft. . . . From the depths of my exile, I never cease to pray, my eyelids already heavy, my thoughts already frozen, arrested at the moment when you abandoned your home and body, when you forgot love and destiny, the passion of that destiny that my will forged, but of which you were not worthy. . . ."

My father's voice was followed by the enlarged, hideous image of a face ravaged by illness. It was my mother's. She looked at me, rooting me to the spot. I thought her lips were moving, but no sound came out of them. Her wrinkles shifted and gave her an expression of great hilarity; her eyes were white, as if turned to the sky. I even glimpsed in them some tenderness, a sort of fatalistic resignation, a wandering wound that lodged sometimes in her heart, sometimes in the visible parts of her body. It was a long time since she had heard her husband's voice. She had blocked up her ears with hot wax. She had suffered, but preferred total silence to that soulless, merciless, pitiless voice. Her madness had begun with that deafness; "a little death," she said, but at the time I understood neither her gesture nor her silence. Disfigured, she had abandoned everything. Since she could neither read nor write, she spent her time shut up in her dark room, where she murmured incomprehensible things to herself. Her daughters had abandoned her. I had ignored her. Now I don't know what to do.

In the night, I lie there with my eyes open so as not to see her gloomy face; I sigh, but I hear my mother's body panting. I shut my eyes; I am surrounded by a harsh light, confronted with the image of that suffering woman; I am powerless, unable to move, but above all I cannot open my eyes and escape that vision.

I know that face will be there as long as my mother suffers, until some kindly hand comes and delivers her from the prison in which she has been slowly engulfed, where she has dug her own grave, where she lay down, awaiting death or a sparrow come from paradise, wrapped in silence, wishing to be the witness and victim of a life that she could not live.

There are women in this country who step over all barriers, dominate, command, guide, trample others underfoot—such a woman was Um Abbas. Men—and not only her son—feared her. She claimed to have had two husbands at the same time. One day she even showed me two marriage certificates in which there was no mention of divorce—a rare, strange thing, but not really surprising to anybody who knew her.

I also mention the face of this strong, brutal woman in order to offset my mother's presence in that disturbing darkness. How can I escape her? One answer occurred to me right away—through love. Impossible. Pity perhaps, but not love.

A hedge of very green reeds lifts me up: a garden of ferns and other greenery reaches me in that endless night. It goes some way to driving away my mother's face, though without making it disappear entirely, and fills me with a flood of light and perfume. I breathe deeply, knowing that this is only a brief interlude in my ordeal. The grass has penetrated everywhere in the space I am sitting in, which is subject not to ghosts but to beings who demand justice, love, memory.

When the garden has slowly withdrawn, I find myself in a bare terrain, with my mother, who is calm for the time being. In a corner, scarcely lit, is a small wheelchair. I see it from behind. Perhaps there is no one in it. I don't move. I wait. No point in provoking mishap. It begins to head for me. I see a forehead marked by many vertical lines; a mouth, twisted in the final death agony, the mark of the last cry; the tiny, stiff body; the eyes open, fixed on some indeterminate point. The wheelchair moves away, goes in circles, stops, withdraws, then bears down on me. I hold out my hands to stop it; it brakes, then sets off again, as if controlled by some hidden hand or operated automatically. I observe the merry-go-round and say nothing. I try to recognize the person who is amusing himself in this way, but the movement is so rapid that I catch glimpses only of vague flashes. I think of Fatima and see her corpse once more. The forehead is not hers. Death has changed it. She is now floating on a lagoon, which has flooded the bare, white terrain. She says nothing. I cannot understand the meaning of all this commotion.

14

Salem

It is now eight months and twenty-four days since the
storyteller disappeared. Those who came to listen to him
no longer turn up. They have dispersed since the thread
that brought them together has been broken. In fact, the
storyteller, like the acrobats and other vendors of odd objects, had to leave the large piece of ground, which the
local authorities, at the instigation of young technocratic
town planners, has "cleaned up" in order to build a musical
fountain. Where, every Sunday, jets of water will play to
the accompaniment of the bo-bo-pa-*pa* of Beethoven's Fifth
Symphony. The square has been cleared. There are no
more snake charmers, no more donkey trainers or appren-
tice acrobats, no more beggars come up from the South after
the drought. No more charlatans, no more swallowers
of nails and needles, no more drunken dancers or one-
legged circus performers, no more magic jellabas with fifteen pockets, no more kids simulating an accident under
a truck, no more men dressed in blue selling herbs and

hyena's liver to ward off evil, no more ex-prostitutes turned fortunetellers, no more black tents enclosing the mystery to be kept preciously in the depths of one's memory, no more flute players delighting young maidens, no more shops where people ate steamed sheep heads, no more toothless, blind singers who have no voice but insist on singing about the passionate love of Quaiss and Leila, no more men showing erotic pictures to the sons of good families; the square has emptied. No longer a merry-go-round, it is now simply a piece of ground cleared for a useless fountain. They have even shifted the bus station to the other end of the town. Only the Club Méditerranée has remained in place.

The storyteller died of a broken heart; his body was found near a dried-up spring. He was clutching a book to his breast—the manuscript found at Marrakesh, Ahmed-Zahra's private journal. The police left the body at the morgue for the regulation length of time, then put it at the disposal of the capital's medical school. As for the manuscript, it went up in flames with the old storyteller's clothes. We shall never know the end of this story. And yet a story is written to be told to the end.

This is what Salem, Amar, and Fatuma said. These three, all elderly, with time on their hands, had been meeting ever since the land was cleared and the storyteller died, in a tiny café on the edge of the site, which the local authority's bulldozers had spared because it belonged to the mokaddam's son.

The storyteller's most faithful followers, they found it hard to accept that everything had suddenly come to an end. Salem, a black, the son of a slave brought back from Senegal by a rich merchant in the early years of the century, offered to continue the story. Amar and Fatuma were not enthusiastic: "Why you and not us?"

"Because I've lived and worked in a big house like the one described by the storyteller. There were only girls, and a vague cousin not richly endowed by nature, a dwarf, came to the house from time to time. He would stay for several days without going out. The girls had a good time. We could hear them laughing all the time, without knowing why. In fact, the dwarf had an enormous sexual appetite. He came and satisfied them one after another and left with money and gifts. Being black and a slave's son, I had no luck with them. . . ."

"But that's got nothing to do with our story."

"Yes, yes, it has. You see . . . Let me tell you what happened to Zahra, Lalla Zahra, and then you will tell me your story, each in turn."

"But you aren't a storyteller. You don't have the gifts of Si Abdel Malek, may God have his soul. . . ."

"I may not possess his skill, but I know things, so listen:

This whole story began on the day of Ahmed's death, because if he had not died no one would have learned of these events. First, the corpse washers, called in during the morning by the seven sisters, who had met in the old, dilapidated house, had no sooner gone into the room to wash the corpse than they ran out again, cursing the family. Women washers, not men, should have been called, because, after all, Ahmed's body had remained that of a woman. The sisters know nothing of this. Only the father, the mother, and the midwife had shared the secret. You can imagine how shocked the seven sisters and the rest of the family were. The old uncle, Fatima's father, was there, in a wheelchair. He was weeping with rage. Gesticulating with his stick, he demanded to be taken into the room where the dead man lay in order to beat him. So he was taken to see Ahmed's body, which he struck with his stick so violently that he lost his balance and fell on top of him. He yelled out for help, because his jellaba had got caught in the corpse's teeth. He pulled and pulled at it, moving Ahmed's head. The wheelchair, which had fallen on top of the old uncle, held him in an indecent position, with his entire body stretched out over Ahmed. However, it was a ridiculous sight, not an erotic one. The servants ran in to rescue the invalid, who was frothing at the mouth. They did their best to stifle their laughter. When they had released their employer, they saw Ahmed's female body and uttered a cry of astonishment, then took away the old man, who was in a profound state of shock.

The funeral took place in secret. Strange to say, the body was buried at night, a practice forbidden by our religion. It is even said that the body was cut up and given to the animals at the zoo. But I don't believe this, because I have heard something else. A rumor soon spread that a saint had just been buried in the cemetery, a saint known as the saint of blessed fertility, for he could ensure that women gave birth only to male children. I now realize how legends about saints come about. This one began very soon after his death. Usually a few years have to elapse, and tests are carried out. Our saint had no need of all that. He is now in paradise, and the other day I saw masons building a Marabout tomb, a room around the grave. I asked the laborers what they were doing. One of them said it was for a new saint—a rich, powerful man, who wished to remain anonymous, had ordered the construction of this little shrine.

The architecture is very curious. The room is surmounted not by a single dome, as are most Marabout tombs, but by two domes, which when seen from afar resemble the breasts of a well-endowed woman or, if you'll pardon the image, a pair of fleshy buttocks! The police have already investigated. The whole thing is shrouded in mystery. Since the police were unable to discover the name of the individual who had ordered the building, they are not taking any action; he must, they are telling themselves, be something of a big shot. Anyway, I'm sure he's someone important, someone with money and influence. But why would he give our character this posthumous recognition? Did he know him before? Was he aware of the drama of his life? Was he a member of the family? There is no answer to any of these questions.

Personally, I think it is more interesting to try to understand how our character's destiny is continuing beyond death, in a sainthood fabricated entirely by some mysterious individual, than to guess how he escaped from the circus troupe or even how he died and at whose hand.

But I do know what happened during the last months of his life. Though I should say "suspect," not "know."

She still slept curled up, her mouth tightly shut and her fists between her thighs. She told herself that the hour of damnation had come and that those whom, by the nature of things, she had hurt would take their revenge. She no longer had a mask to protect herself. She had been handed over, defenseless, to a brutal world.

Abbas, the circus boss, was a brute, physically and mentally. He weighed over two hundred pounds and took every opportunity to demonstrate his physical strength. He beat the circus boys with a belt. He often forgot to wash and shave, but spent hours arranging his mustache, which covered up a good part of his face. He said he had the strength of a Turk, the faith of a Berber, the appetite of a falcon of Arabia, the finesse of a European, and the soul of a vagabond of the plains.

In fact, he was a tribesman from the mountains who had been cursed by his father and expelled from the tribe along with his mother, who practiced black magic. Banished by their family and clan, the son and mother joined together to continue their evil deeds. Utter lack of scruple, a determination to harm others—to exploit them, to rob them, even to murder them—made them a dangerous couple, ready to do anything, capable of anything that would serve their purposes. They seldom remained in the same place for long. They were constantly on the move, not to avoid the police—whom they bribed wherever they went—but to find new victims.

Abbas, so violent, domineering, and contemptuous with his circus employees, became a gentle little boy, bowing his head and lowering his eyes, when confronted by his mother or anyone representing authority, and immediately offered his services. He acted as an informer and a supplier of virgins or young boys to the kaid, the village chief, or the police chief. His relationship with his mother was a very strange one. He often slept in the same bed as she, laying his head between her breasts. It was said that he had never been weaned and that his mother had gone on feeding him at the breast well beyond puberty. His mother loved him violently, but would beat him with a stick studded with nails and tell him that he was her man, her only man. She was training him so that he could go back to the mountain and bring misfortune on the whole family, especially on his father. He acquired skills, drew up plans, prepared formulas for poisoning the food and even the well, the only well in the village. He was possessed by the idea of a total massacre. He saw himself clambering up the heaped corpses of the tribe, triumphant, his mother on his back. Over his shoulder she would admire the work of her child, whom she had reared in her own image.

They both dreamed of that precise moment; the mother had admitted to him that the prospect filled her with joy. She got up and jumped onto her son's back and he galloped around the room. The son got a huge erection, put down his mother, and ran off to relieve himself outside, behind a tent, preferably the one in which Zahra slept. One day he battered down the door, woke up the girls who were with Zahra, and sent them packing. He was now alone with Zahra. His trousers were already open: with one hand he held his member, with the other a knife. He yelled at Zahra to let him have his way with her: "From behind, you fool, give me your ass, it's all you've got, you've got no breasts to speak of, and I don't want your vagina. Give me your ass. . . . I'll give you the best time you've had in your life. You do it by yourself; I'll teach you how to do it with others. . . ."

He threw himself on her, but even before penetrating her, he ejaculated. With a furious cry, he slashed her back with the knife. Abbas left, cursing her, and went back to cry between his mother's breasts.

A few moments later, he came back with handcuffs, attached Zahra's arms to the bars of the window, and raped her with an old piece of wood.

Zahra was no longer Princess of Love; she no longer danced; she was no longer a man or a woman, but a circus animal whom the old woman exhibited in a cage. With her hands tied, her dress torn to the waist to reveal her small breasts, Zahra had given up the use of speech. She wept, and the tears flowed down her face, on which the beard had started growing: she had become a bearded lady, visited from every corner of the city. People's curiosity knew no bounds. They paid dear to get near the cage. Some threw peanuts at her, others razor blades, others spat at her in disgust. Zahra brought Abbas and his mother a lot of money. Her silence, however, disturbed them. One night the old woman untied her, gave her something to eat, and took her to the bathroom. The old woman insisted on washing Zahra once a week. As she was pouring water over Zahra's body, she stroked her, felt her vagina, and said such things to her as "It's a good thing we're here. We saved you! All your life you've been usurping someone else's identity, probably that of a man you murdered. Now you'd better obey us and do as you're told. I don't know what my fool of a son sees in you. You've got no breasts, you're thin, your buttocks are tiny and hard—even a boy has more flesh on him than you. Anyway, when I put my hand on your skin I feel nothing. It's like wood. Whereas with the other girls, even the ugly ones, I get some pleasure. If you keep refusing to speak, I'll hand you over to the police. Our police have a way of making the dumb speak. . . ."

One night with a full moon, Zahra felt that Abbas was going to attack her again. With her free hand she picked up two razor blades that had been thrown into the cage by spectators. She undressed and put the two blades in a rag, which she placed between her buttocks; lying on her belly, she awaited the brute's visit. She had read in an old magazine that during the Indochinese war women had used this method to kill enemy soldiers who raped them. It was also a form of suicide.

Abbas's body fell on Zahra's like a ton weight. His member was cut. Yelling with pain and rage, he strangled her. Zahra died at dawn, and the rapist later died from loss of blood.

That is how Ahmed died. That is how Zahra's brief life came to an end.

Salem looked very moved by his own story. He gave a long sigh, got up, and said to Amar and Fatuma: "Excuse me. I didn't want to tell you the end of the story, but when I found out about it, I was so overcome that I looked everywhere for someone to tell it to, so I wouldn't be the sole witness of such a tragedy. Now I feel better. I feel relieved."

"Sit down!" Amar cut in. "You're not going to get out of it like that! Your story is terrible. I'm sure you made it all up and that you identified as much with Abbas as with the wretched Zahra. You're a pervert. You dream of raping young girls or boys and, because you're ashamed of it, you punish yourself in the Asiatic manner. . . . I know the end of this story. I found the manuscript the storyteller was reading to us. I shall bring it along tomorrow. I salvaged it from the nurses at the morgue."

Fatuma said nothing. She gave a faint smile, got up, and gestured as if to say, "See you tomorrow."

15

Amar

On that day, some clouds had gathered in the sky, forming
an almost perfect circle, and were slowly being washed by
a color somewhere between mauve and red. A light mist
still hung over the city. People were strolling up and down
the great avenues with no particular purpose in mind. Some
had sat down in the café. They were talking—not about
anything of great importance, just the small things of
everyday life. They were watching the girls go by. Some
made vulgar comments, about one woman's walk or about
the low-slung backside of another. Others were reading
or rereading a newspaper; from time to time they men-
tioned the spread of male prostitution in the city; they
pointed their fingers at a European tourist flanked by two
handsome boys.

People like to talk about others. Here they love sexual
gossip. They spread it all the time. Among those who were
making fun of an English homosexual a little while ago,
I know some who would be quite willing to make love

with him. They find it easier to do than to talk or write about it. Books that deal with prostitution in the country are forbidden, but nothing is done to give work to the girls who arrive from the country, nor is anything done about their pimps. So people talk about it in the cafés. They let their imagination loose on the sights that cross the boulevard. In the evening they watch an interminable Egyptian soap opera on television. "The Call of Love" depicts men and women loving one another, hating one another, tearing one another apart, and never touching one another. I tell you, my friends, we live in a hypocritical society. I don't have to say any more: you know very well how corruption has done its work and is still, slowly but surely, undermining our bodies and souls. I am very fond of the Arabic word for "corruption." It is applied to materials that lose their substance and virtue—like wood, for example, which retains its outer surface and appearance but is hollow. There is nothing inside; it is undermined from within; tiny insects have nibbled away at everything under the bark.

My friends, do not jostle me too violently; I am only an empty carcass; inside there are still a heart and lungs that continue to do their work. They are more indignant than tired. And I am lost.

Yesterday, after the story that Salem brought us, I went to the mosque, not to pray, but to try to understand what is happening to us. Imagine, I was woken several times by individuals, some sort of night watchmen, I suppose. They searched me and checked my identity. I wanted to say to them: The Islam that I carry inside me cannot be found; I am a man who has lived alone, and religion does not really interest me. But if I talked about Ibn Arabi or

El Hallaj, I would certainly have got myself into trouble. They would have thought these were political leaders in exile, Muslim brothers wanting to seize power in the country. So I got up and went home. Fortunately the children weren't there. They must have been all out in the vacant lot, playing in the stones and dust.

I thought hard and long about poor Ahmed. I shall not call him Zahra, because he signed his manuscript with a single initial, the letter "A." Of course, it might have been Aysha, Amina, Atika, Alia, Assia. . . . But let's say he meant Ahmed. It is true he left the house and abandoned everything. He was tempted to go along with the circus adventure, but I believe he did something else.

The mother and her brutish son, their faces exuding hatred—hatred of others and of themselves—were no longer capable of pulling off any of their schemes. They tried to get Ahmed involved in some scheme, but they clearly lacked all credibility, since they were constantly cheating each other and indulging in violent arguments. Anyway, what finally made Ahmed decide to run away was a fight between mother and son with cold steel, about a lost jar in which the old woman had preserved a powdered hyena's brain. She provoked her son to anger, shouting: "Son of a whore, son of a queer, you're not a man; come and fight, come and defend the little virility I was kind enough to give you at birth."

"If you're a whore," he replied, "I'm only your son, and whores' sons are less rotten than their mothers."

"Where did you put the black jar? You made me lose a really big deal there. I'm sure you gave it to that old queen who gives you his ass. You're the unworthy son of a great lady. . . ."

"I don't want to fight—not with you!"

She threw a dagger at him; it grazed his shoulder. The son began to cry and beg his mother to forgive him. He was really ugly. They were both unbearably ugly, devoid of all dignity. They were not like mother and son, but two monsters who aroused such horror in Ahmed that he took flight, cursing the invisible hand that had brought them together. Still cursing her son, the old woman took chase. She nearly caught Ahmed, but slipped on a wet paving stone, which saved him from the old witch's clutches.

Ahmed would never have imagined that such a relationship could exist between a mother and a son. He remembered his own relations with his parents and deeply regretted his harsh behavior toward them, his obdurate silences, and his unreasonable demands. He told himself that he could not master the hate that kept him from his poor mother, or the passionate feelings aroused in him by his father, whom he both admired and feared. He began to detest the cynical sham of the marriage to his poor cousin.

All night he wandered through the city. At dawn he went to the cemetery and looked for Fatima's grave. He found it, neglected, stuck between two large gray stones. When he thought of her, it was with remorse, something he had not felt for a long time. It was as if he had come home after a long absence, a difficult journey or some long illness. As he stood contemplating that grave, the image of Fatima gradually became blurred, her voice inaudible, her cries lost in the wind; his memories were gently crumbling away.

Ahmed hated cemeteries. He couldn't understand why they weren't covered up or hidden away. They were unhealthy places. There was no point in preserving the illusion of a present. Even our memory plays us false, makes fun of us to the extent of fabricating memories with people who never existed.

He began to doubt whether Fatima had ever existed, and refused to believe that he had come to her grave to pray for her soul. In fact, his perception had been seriously affected by lack of sleep and nervous exhaustion. He left the cemetery as if blown by a sudden gust of wind, or as if someone were pushing him from behind. He did not resist. He walked backward, stumbled over a stone, and found himself laid out in a grave that exactly fitted his body. He found it hard to get up. For a moment he thought of staying there and sleeping. Perhaps death would come and take him in her arms, gently, without regret. He would remain in that position, as if to tame death, to familiarize himself with the dampness of the earth, and thus to become fond of her. But the wind was too strong. He got up.

Ahmed left, bitter and sad. His first attempts at seduction were rejected by death, or at least by the wind that conveyed it from one place to another. He told himself that he belonged neither to life nor to death, just as he had lived the first part of his history as neither a man nor a woman. The worst thing was, he no longer knew what kind of a creature he was. No mirror returned his image. They were all dulled: only darkness, with a few hatchings of light, appeared in mirrors.

He knew that his case was hopeless, now that he could no longer even find a face in which he could see himself, eyes that would say to him: "You've changed. You're not the same person as you were yesterday. You have white hairs at your temples; you don't smile any more; your eyes are growing dim; you've got snot hanging from your nose.

You're finished, done for; you no longer exist; you're a mistake, an absence, a handful of ashes, a few pebbles, shards of glass, a little pile of sand, a hollow tree trunk; your face is disappearing; don't try to hold on to it, let it go; you'll be better off without it, one face less. Let your head drop off, roll along the ground, collect a little dust and a few blades of grass, let it roll to the other end of your thoughts; don't worry if it ends up in a circus; it will roll until it no longer feels anything. . . ."

A charlatan to whom he confided his misfortune offered to get him an Indian mirror, specially designed for such cases as his. "With this mirror you will see your face and your thoughts. You will see what others do not see when they look at you. It's a mirror for the depths of the soul, for the visible and the invisible. It's a rare device used by the princes of the Orient to unravel riddles. Believe me, my friend, it will save you, for in it you will see the stars that guard the Empire of the Secret. . . ."

"Who told you," Ahmed replied, "that I want to be saved? I'd be happier if I lost my face and its image forever. Already, after a long night of thinking and wandering, I pass my hand over my cheeks and feel nothing—my hand moves over a void. It's a feeling you can't understand, unless you're a great smoker of kief. And even then you have to have had trouble with your name and been bothered by having a double. But all that's beyond you. Go away, now; all I need is silence and an immense layer of darkness. I don't need a mirror. Anyway, I don't believe in your story. When I was a child, we used to play with those Indian mirrors—we used to start fires with them!"

He continued to wander around for long time. His physical and mental state left him like a shadow that passed without arousing the slightest attention. He preferred this indifference, because, as he had observed, "I am on the path of anonymity and deliverance."

One might say that, at this stage, he had been lost sight of, but nobody was sufficiently interested in him to lose sight of him. What he wanted was to lose sight of himself, once and for all, and not to be driven this way and that by the flood of time.

I don't know how he survived, whether he ate or not, whether he slept or not. His last observations were extremely vague. Was he still in this country, or had he managed to stow away on some cargo ship setting out for the ends of the earth? I mention this because at one point he speaks of "the darkness buffeted by strong waves."

I imagine that body, which could no longer be imprisoned in another body, on the high seas, not in one of those sleazy bars where the soul is diluted in bad wine.

When he left the house and abandoned the stability of home life, he was ready for any adventure, though he did have a wish to put an end to the whole painful comedy of his life. This is what he wrote at the time:

Death has settled many unresolved questions. My parents are no longer there to remind me that I bear a secret. It is time I knew who I am. I know I have a woman's body, even if a slight doubt persists as to appearances. I have a woman's body; that is to say, I have a woman's sexual organs, though they were never used. I'm an old maid who doesn't even have the right to share the fears of an old maid. I behave like a man—or, to be more precise, I have been taught to act and to think as one who is naturally superior to women. Everything allows me to do this: religion, the Koran, society, tradition, the family, the country . . . and myself. . . .

I have small breasts—breasts that were repressed from adolescence—but a man's voice. My voice is low, because it might betray me. From now on, I shall no longer speak. Or, rather, I shall speak with my hand over my mouth, as if I had a toothache.

I have a delicate face, but my beard grows.

I have benefited from the laws of inheritance that give men privileges over women: I have inherited twice as much as my sisters. But this money no longer interests me: I have left it to them. I would like to leave this house without having the slightest trace of the past follow me. I would like to leave so that I might be born again, to be born at twenty-five years of age, without parents or family, but with a woman's first name, with a woman's body, rid forever of these lies.

I may not live very long. I know that my destiny is to be suddenly interrupted because, more or less in spite of myself, I have played at deceiving God and his prophets. Not my father, whose instrument I was, an opportunity for revenge, an attempt to defy a curse. I was aware of acting to some extent.

Even now I sometimes imagine what kind of life I would have had if I had been simply an ordinary girl, one girl more, the eighth, another source of anxiety and misfortune. I believe I would not have been able to live and accept what my sisters and the other girls in this country have to endure. I don't believe I am better than they, but I sense within me such determination, such rebellious strength, that I would probably have upset everything.

Ah! How angry I am at myself for not unveiling my

identity sooner and smashing the mirrors that kept me away from life. I would have been a woman living alone, deciding quite calmly what to do with my solitude. I mean a solitude chosen, elected, experienced as a desire for freedom, not a retirement imposed by family and clan. I know that in this country a single woman is doomed to every kind of rejection. In a moral, well-structured society, not only is everyone in his place, but there is absolutely no place for him or her, especially her, who, consciously or erroneously, betrays the established order. A single woman, unmarried or divorced, an unmarried mother, is someone exposed to every kind of rejection. A child born in the shadow of the law, born of a union that is not recognized, is destined at best for the orphanage, where the bad seeds, the seeds of pleasure—in other words, of infidelity and shame—are reared. A secret prayer will be said that this child should not be one of the hundred thousand babies who die each year, through lack of proper care, through lack of food, or by God's curse. This child will have no name; it will be a son or a daughter of the street and of sin, and will have to endure every form of misfortune.

Arrangements should be made to have, outside each town, a deep pond into which the bodies of these unwanted babies might be thrown. It could be called the pond of deliverance. Mothers could go there, preferably at night, wrap their progeny around a stone that some well-intentioned hand would give them, and, with a final sob, set the child down; hidden hands from under the water would drag the child to the bottom and drown it. All this would be done with the full knowledge of the community, but it would be indecent—indeed, forbidden—to speak of it, even to mention the subject, however indirectly.

My country's violence is also to be found in those closed eyes, in those diverted looks, in those silences, which stem from resignation rather than indifference.

Today I am a single woman. An old single woman. Now, at the age of twenty-five, I consider that my old age has at least half a century to run. Two lives with two perceptions and two faces, but the same dreams, the same profound solitude. I don't think I'm innocent. I even think I've become rather dangerous. I no longer have anything to lose, and there is so much in me to repair. . . . I'm suspicious of my capacity for anger and destructive hatred. Nothing can hold me back any more. I'm just a little afraid of what I might do. I'm afraid because I don't know exactly what I'm going to do, but I've made up my mind to do it.

I could, of course, have remained shut up in the cage from which I gave orders and managed the affairs of the family. I could have been content with the status of an invisible, powerful man. I could even have built a still higher room, to have a better view of the city. But my life, my nights, my breathing, my desires would have been condemned. Ever since, I have had a strong loathing for the desert, for the desert island, for the tiny house isolated in the woods. I want to go out, to see people, to breathe the bad smells of this country as well as the perfumes of its fruits and flowers. To go out, to be jostled, to be in the midst of the crowd, and to feel a man's hand clumsily groping for my buttocks. Many women find this very disagreeable. I can understand them. For me, it would be the first anonymous hand laid on my back or hips. I would not turn around, so that I would not see the face of the man who was touching me. If I saw it, I would probably be horrified. But bad manners or vulgar gestures can sometimes have a touch of poetry about them, just enough not to arouse one's indignation. . . .

I now understand why my father did not let me go out; he arranged circumstances to thicken the mystery around my existence. At one point he lost confidence in me. I might have betrayed him—gone out naked, for instance. People would have said, "It's a madwoman!" They would have covered me and brought me home. That idea haunted me. But what is the use of causing a scandal? My father was ill, my mother enclosed in her silence. My sisters lived an orderly, ordinary life.

After my parents' death, I felt a sense of deliverance, a new freedom. Now nothing held me in that house. I could go out at last, leave and never come back.

I had reached the point of yearning for amnesia, of wanting to burn my memories one after another, or gather them up like a pile of firewood, tie them together with a transparent thread or a spider web, and get rid of them in the market place, selling them for a little oblivion, for a little peace and quiet. But that would be too easy a solution.

To go out, to walk away, head held back, looking at the sky to catch the rise of a star at dusk, and to give up thinking. To choose some quiet hour, some secret road, a gentle light, a landscape where loving creatures without a past, without a history, would sit around as in those Persian miniatures where everything seems marvelous, outside time. Ah! If only I could step over that prickly hedge, that moving wall that keeps just ahead of me and bars my way. If only I could cross it, at the risk of a few scratches, and take my place in the eleventh-century miniature! Angels' hands would set me down on the precious carpet in silence, without disturbing the old storyteller, a sage who practices love with great delicacy. I see him there stroking the hips of a young girl, happy to give herself to him, without fear, without violence, with love and modesty. . . .

So many books have been written about bodies, pleasures, perfumes, tenderness, the sweetness of love between man and woman in Islam—ancient books that nobody reads nowadays. Where has the spirit of that poetry gone? To go out and forget, to head for places withdrawn from time. And wait. Before, I expected nothing—or, rather, my life was governed by my father's strategy; I accumulated things without having to wait. Now I shall have the leisure to wait. For anything or anybody. I shall know that waiting may be a ceremony, an enchantment, and that I shall make some face or hand emerge out of the distance; I shall stroke it, seated before the horizon with its constantly shifting lines and colors; I shall watch my visitor leave; thus I will be given the wish to die slowly before that ever-receding sky. . . .

That, my friends, is how our character died: before the sky, before the sea, surrounded by images, in the sweetness of the words he was writing, in the tenderness of the thoughts he cherished. I believe he never left his room high up on the terrace of the big house. He let himself die there, surrounded by old Arabic and Persian manuscripts on love, drowned by the call of the desire that he imagined, without ever being visited by anybody. He locked his door during the day. At night he slept on the terrace and conversed with the stars. His body was of little importance to him; he let it waste away. He wanted to conquer time. I think he succeeded in the last stage of his life, when he reached the highest degree of contemplation. I think he knew that ecstatic beatitude one sometimes feels when contemplating a starry sky. He must have had a very gentle death. His eyes resting on that distant horizon, he must have gone over the long ordeal, or at least the error that was his life. What I am going to read you now is not to be found in the manuscript; it springs from my own imagination:

I am going on tiptoe. I don't want to be heavy, in case the angels, as is said in the Koran, come to carry me off to heaven. I have emptied my body and set fire to my memory. I was born in the midst of fabricated celebrations. I leave in silence. I was, as the poet says, "the last and most solitary of human beings, deprived of love and friendship, and in that much inferior to the most imperfect of the animals." I was a mistake, and in life I have known nothing but masks and lies. . . .

Amar's narrative was followed by a long silence. Salem and Fatuma looked convinced; they regarded each other but said nothing. Then, after a while, Salem, embarrassed, tried to justify his own version of the story:

"This character is in himself an act of violence; his destiny, his life are really inconceivable. You can't get out of it by making some psychological pirouette. To put it crudely, you must admit that Ahmed is not one of nature's mistakes, but a social deviation. Anyway, what I mean is, he isn't someone attracted by his own sex. With his desires totally crushed, I think only a great act of violence—a suicide with lots of blood—can bring this story to an appropriate end."

"You've read too many books," said Amar. "That's an intellectual's explanation. But I ask the question: what is there in this unfinished story that is of such interest to us idle, disillusioned folk? You, the son of slaves, have spent your life in study. You'd have liked to know what a free life was like when you were twenty—but at twenty your parents were doing their best to spare you the misfortunes *they* had had to endure. As for me, I'm an old, retired schoolteacher, tired of this country—or, to be more precise, by those who mistreat and disfigure it. I wonder what I found so interesting in this story. I suppose it was, first of all, its enigmatic quality, then the comment it provides on our society, which is very harsh. I know it doesn't seem that way, but there's such violence in our relationships that a crazy story about a man with a woman's body is a means of carrying that violence to its limit. That's what fascinates us. You, Fatuma, you've said nothing. What is your opinion?"

"Yes, I've said nothing, because in this country a woman is used to keeping quiet; if she does speak out, that's an act of violence in itself. I'm old now, which is why I can sit around with you. Thirty years ago, or when I was about thirty, do you think I would have dared to be seen with you in a café? I'm free because I'm old and wrinkled. I'm allowed to speak because nothing I say can be of any importance. The risks are minimal. Yet it still feels odd to be here today, sitting in a café, listening to you, and talking. We hardly know one another. You know nothing about me. If you remember, it was I who suggested that we come and meet in this café after the storyteller's disappearance. It was I who spoke first. You didn't notice. Common enough, you might say—after all, an old woman

. . . But it's not so common as all that! An old woman has to stay at home and look after her grandchildren; I'm neither a mother nor a grandmother. Perhaps I'm the only childless old woman alive. I live alone. I have a little income. I travel. I read—I learned to read at school; I think I was the only girl in the whole school. My father was proud of me; he said, 'I'm not ashamed of having daughters!' ''

Fatuma stopped for a moment, shielded her face with part of her headscarf, and lowered her eyes. It was difficult to tell whether she was embarrassed by what she was saying or by the presence of someone. In fact, she was trying to avoid someone's gaze. A short, rather well-dressed man had stopped in front of the café. His eyes moved from Fatuma, who kept her head lowered, to the back of the café. He walked up to our table and said, "Well, Hajja! Don't you recognize me? We were at Mecca together. I'm Hajji Britel, the quick, efficient bird!"

Amar asked him to leave them alone. The man went off, muttering something like "My memory plays tricks on me, and yet I'm sure it was she. . . ."

Fatuma unveiled her face. This interruption had disturbed her. She remained silent for a while, then, after a deep sigh, said: "In life one should carry two faces. It would be good to have a spare face—or, better still, no face at all. We would just be voices, as if we were all blind. . . . Well, my friends, I invite you to come to my place tomorrow so that we can hear the end of our story. I live in a room at the orphanage. I'll expect you at sundown. Come just before—you'll see how beautiful the sky is from my room. . . ."

16

Fatuma

Men! There is a piety that I love and seek, the piety of memory. I like it because it asks no questions. I know you possess this quality. Thus I shall forestall your questions and satisfy your curiosity.

You are sitting on the floor, with your backs to the wall, facing the mountain. A band of cloud is hiding its summit. Very soon the colors will slowly mingle with the clouds. They will provide a spectacle for the eye and spirit that can wait for it.

As the poet says, "One can only forget time by making use of it."

Before, time made use of me, and in the end I forgot myself. My body, my soul, the fire I could raise, the dawn in which I took refuge, all that left me indifferent. Everything was silent around me: the water, the spring, the moon, the street.

And I come from far away, very far; I have tramped endless roads, crossed frozen territories and endless spaces filled with shadows and tents. Countries and centuries have passed before my eyes. My feet still remember them. I keep my memory on the soles of my feet. Was it I who moved forward, or the earth that moved beneath my feet? No, I made up those journeys, those nights without dawns, as I lay in a tall, narrow, circular room. A room overlooking the terrace. The terrace was on a hill and the hill was painted on a piece of pale-red silk. I had taken up residence at the top of the house, the windows and door closed. Light was undesirable. I felt freer in the darkness. I organized my journeys from bits and pieces of travelers' accounts. If I had been a man I would have said, "*I* am Ibn Batuta!" But I'm only a woman and live in a room at the height of a hanging tomb.

I went to Mecca, more out of curiosity than faith. I was drowned by that horde dressed in white, jostled and crushed. There was not a great deal of difference between my bare room and the great mosque. At no moment did I lose consciousness. On the contrary, everything brought me back to myself and to my small world, where my ties were devouring and exhausting me. It was strictly forbidden to leave the pilgrimage before its end, but I couldn't stand it any longer. I had lost track of the potter, the man who was supposed to supervise and protect my virtue. For the first time I wanted to put an end to it. Death means so little in those places.

I had within me, in my breast, something that had been put there by familiar hands: I held back a long, painful cry. I knew it wasn't mine, yet I had a sense that it was up to me whether I uttered that cry, a cry that would shatter the compact body of the crowd of worshipers, that would make the mountains surrounding the holy places shake;

that cry, imprisoned within my rib cage, was that of a woman. The need to expel it from my body became more and more urgent as the crowd surrounding me grew larger. I knew, intuitively again, that this woman had left it inside me just before dying. She was young and sick. She probably suffered from asthma or epilepsy—I'm not sure. In any case, I had to have reached that place of prayer and meditation to feel this desire to rend the heavens with my cry, a deep cry of which I possessed the seeds but not the causes. I felt quite capable of making that cry, thus doing justice to the absent one, the sick creature who had lived so little and so poorly. Later I wondered: Why did that cry find refuge in me and not in a man, for example? An inner voice answered that the cry should have been in a man's breast and there had been a mistake—or, rather, the young woman had preferred to give it to a woman, capable of feeling the same suffering as herself. I moved on through the crowd, my chest thrust out, pregnant with that cry.

As the pilgrims dispersed, I no longer felt a need to cry out; the tension that had driven me forward abated. I left Mecca without regret and took the first available boat. I love traveling by boat. To be on the ocean, far from all ties, not to know where I'm going, to be suspended without past or future, to be in the immediate moment, surrounded by that blue immensity, to watch the thin envelope of the sky at night, when so many stars thread their way in and out of it; to feel myself in the gentle grip of a blind sensation that slowly turns into a melody, something between melancholy and inner joy—that was what I liked. That ship reconciled me with the interrupted wedding of silence.

My pilgrimage, even if left unfinished, had freed me:

when I returned to my own country, I did not go back to my own home. I had no wish to return to that old, dilapidated house, where the rest of my family still lived in intermittent misfortune I abandoned my room and my books without regret. At night I slept in a mosque. Crouching in my jellaba, the hood pulled down over my face, I could be taken for a man, some mountain tribesman lost in the city. Then it occurred to me that I could disguise myself as a man. It wouldn't take a lot: it was just a matter of arranging appearances. When I was young and rebellious, I used to amuse myself by changing my image. I have always been slim, which made it easier. It was an extraordinary experience to pass from one state to another. I would change my image, change my face, but keep the same body, and exult in wearing that mask.

And then everything froze; the moment became a room, the room became a sunny day, time a few old bones left in this cardboard box. In this box are old, odd shoes, a handful of unused nails, a Singer sewing machine that turns of its own volition, an airman's glove snatched from a corpse, a caught spider, a razor blade, a glass eye, and, of course, the inevitable worn old mirror, which has shed all its images; indeed, all the objects in the box belong only to its own imagination; it no longer gives out objects, for it has emptied itself during a long absence. . . .

I now know that the key to our story is to be found among these old things. I daren't rummage among them for fear of having my hand snatched by mechanical jaws, which, though rusty, still work; they don't come from the mirror, but from its double. I forgot to mention that; I didn't actually forget—I was superstitious. Never mind— we won't leave this room without finding the key, and for

130

that it will be necessary to mention, if only by allusion, the mirror's double. Don't look for it with your eyes. It's not in this room; at least it's not visible. It's a peaceful garden with oleanders, smooth stones that capture and hold the light; this garden is also frozen, suspended; it is secret, as is the path to it. The few individuals who know of it are those who have familiarized themselves with eternity, who sit out there on a stone that maintains the day intact, held in their gaze. They hold the threads of the beginning and the end. The stone closes off the entrance to the garden; the garden looks out on the sea, and the sea swallows and carries off all the stories that are born and die between the flowers and roots of plants. . . .

In this way I learned to be in the dream and to make of my life an entirely invented story, a tale that recalls what really took place. Is it out of boredom or lassitude that one gives oneself another life, puts it on like a wonderful magic jellaba, a cloak cut out of the sky and studded with stars?

In my retirement, silent and motionless, I witness my country's removal: men and history, plains and mountains, meadows and even the sky are disappearing. Only the women and kids remain. It looks as if they were staying to guard the country, but there's nothing to guard. They come and go, bustle around, get by. Those who have been driven out of the countryside by drought and irrigation projects roam the cities. They beg. They are rejected, humiliated; they go right on begging, snatching what they can. Children . . . Many of them die, far too many, so more are produced, more and still more. To be born a boy is the lesser of two evils. To be born a girl is a calamity, a misfortune that is left at the roadside where death passes by at the end of the day. Oh, I'm not telling you anything new. My story is an old one, from before Islam. My words don't carry much weight—I'm only a woman. I have no tears left. I learned early on that a woman who weeps is lost. I acquired a determination never to be that weeping woman.

I have lived in the illusion of another body, with someone else's clothes and emotions. I deceived everybody right up to the day when I realized that I was deceiving myself. Then I began to look around a bit and what I saw deeply shocked me. How could I live like this, in a glass cage, living a lie, suffering the contempt of others? One cannot move from one life to another simply by crossing a bridge. In my case, I had to rid myself of what I was, enter into oblivion and remove all traces. The opportunity came to me through the kids, all those kids in the shantytowns, thrown out of the schools, without work, without roofs over their heads, without a future, without hope. They had gone out into the streets, first with empty hands, then carrying stones, demanding bread. Yelling any slogan that came into their heads. They could no longer contain their violence. Women and men who were out of work joined them. I was in the street, not knowing what to think. I had no reason to demonstrate with them; I had never known hunger.

As the army fired into the crowd, I happened to find myself with the kids, almost by chance, confronting the forces of order. That day I knew fear and hatred. Everything changed. I got a bullet in my shoulder—some women who were standing at their doors urging on the demonstrators quickly took me in and hid me. When I entered that poor family's house, rescued by women whose children must have been among the crowd, I felt an emotion so strong that I forgot the pain caused by my wound. Tending me with skill and kindness, they kept me for a long time in their home.

The police were looking everywhere for the wounded in order to arrest them. They even mounted guard at the cemeteries. The idea was to cleanse the country of the bad seed in order to prevent new riots. Alas! The country wasn't really cleansed. Other, bloodier riots took place fifteen and twenty years later. . . .

Meanwhile, I had lost the big notebook to which I had consigned my story. I tried to reconstruct it, but in vain; then I went out in search of the story of my earlier life. The rest you know. I admit that I took great pleasure in listening to the storyteller and then to you: it gave me the privilege of reliving certain stages in my life, twenty years later. Now I am very tired. I must ask you to leave me. As you see, I am old, though not so much in years. It's not usual to be the bearer of two lives. I was so afraid of getting mixed up, of losing the thread of the present and being imprisoned in that magical, luminous garden where not a word must enter.

17

The Blind Troubadour

"The secret is sacred, but still ludicrous."

The man who spoke was blind. He did not seem to
have a cane—he just rested his hand on a youth's shoulder.
Tall and thin, wearing a dark suit, he came and sat at the
table with the two men and Fatuma. No one had invited
him. He apologized, adjusted his dark glasses, handed a
coin to his companion, telling him to go amuse himself,
then turned to the woman and said:

It's true! The secret is sacred, but when it becomes ludicrous it's better to be rid of it. Now you'll probably ask
me who I am, who sent me, and why I have landed in
your story like this. Let me explain. . . . No, all you need
to know is that I have spent my life falsifying or altering
other people's stories. Never mind where I come from;
besides, I couldn't tell you whether my first footsteps were
imprinted in the mud of the eastern bank or the western
bank of the river. I like to invent my memories, in ac-

cordance with my listener's face. For in some faces a soul appears, and in others there is only a mask of wrinkled human skin, with nothing behind it. I admit that since becoming blind I have trusted my intuitions. I travel a great deal. Before, I just observed, and recorded what I saw in my head. Now I make the same journeys and I listen; I prick up my ears and learn many things. Strange how the ear works. It seems to me to teach us more about how things are. Sometimes I touch people's faces to detect traces of soul on them. I have spent a lot of time with poets and storytellers. I collected their books, arranged them on my shelves, protected them. I even installed a bed in my place of work. I was a night watchman—and also a watchman during the day. I slept surrounded by all those works; I was their vigilant friend, confidant, and their betrayer.

I come from afar, from another century, thrown into one tale by another tale. Your story, because it is not a translation of reality, interests me. I take it as it is, artificial and painful. When I was young, I was ashamed to be someone who loved only books, not a man of action. So, with my sister I invented stories in which I spent my time fighting ghosts. I moved easily from one story to another, without taking any notice of reality. Today I find myself like a thing set down in your tale, of which I know nothing. I was expelled—though the word is perhaps too strong— from a story that someone whispered in my ear as if I were a dying man who had to be told something poetic or amusing to help him on his way. When I read a book, I settle in it; I can't help it. I said just now that I was a falsifier— I am the biographer of error and lies. I don't know what hands have pushed me in your direction. I believe they are those of your storyteller, who must be a smuggler, a trafficker in words. To help you, I'll tell you where I come from. I'll give you the last sentences of the story that I have lived, and then we may be able to solve the riddle that has brought you together:

In a birdless dawn the magician saw the concentric fire melt on the walls. For an instant he thought of taking refuge in the waters, but he realized at once that death was coming to crown his old age and to absolve him from his labors. He walked on the scraps of fire. They did not bite his flesh, but stroked it and flooded it, without heat and without combustion. With relief, with humiliation, with terror, he realized that he, too, was an apparition, that someone else was dreaming him.

I am that other who has traveled through a country on a bridge linking two dreams. Is it a country, a river, or a desert? How would I know? On this April day in 1957, we are in Marrakesh, in a café whose back room is used to store sacks of fresh olives. We are near a bus station. It stinks of gas. Beggars of all ages come and go around us; they smell even more arid than yesterday. The call to prayer coming from a small mosque that must be at least a hundred and fifty yards to my left does not move them. And why should they rush into the mosque? I understand them, but I can't do anything for them. For a long time my conscience troubled me when I traveled in poor countries. Eventually I got used to it; I no longer feel anything. So we are in Marrakesh, and then in the heart of Buenos Aires, whose streets, I once remarked, "are like the entrails of my soul," and those streets remember me well.

I came bearing a message. One day a woman, probably an Arab—of Islamic culture, in any case—introduced herself to me; she was recommended, it seems, by a friend of whom I had heard no news for a long while. At the time I was not yet blind, but my sight was fading rapidly, and everything seemed to me to be vague and hatched. So I cannot describe this woman's face. She was thin and wore a long dress. What I do remember very well, for it struck me greatly at the time, was her voice. I have rarely heard a voice at once so deep and so shrill. Was it the voice of a man who had undergone an operation on his vocal cords? Or the voice of a woman wounded in her life? Or of a prematurely aged castrated man? It seemed to me at the time that I had already heard that voice in one of the books I had read, perhaps in one of the tales of the *Thousand and One Nights*, the story of a slave girl named Tawaddud who, in order to save her master from ruin, offered to go before the caliph Harun al-Rashid and answer the most difficult questions set by the most learned men—she was endowed with universal knowledge. If she were totally successful, her owner could sell her to the caliph for ten thousand dinars. Of course she emerged from the trial triumphant. Harun al-Rashid took Tawaddud and her master into his court and rewarded them with several thousand dinars.

It is a tale about science and memory. I loved that story, because I, too, was seduced by the knowledge that slave girl possessed, and felt jealous of her rigor and finesse.

Now, I'm almost certain that the woman who visited me had Tawaddud's voice. Yet they were separated by centuries! The slave girl was only fourteen, the woman much older. Still, all that is nothing but coincidence and chance. I forget what she said to me; I wasn't actually listening to her, though I heard her voice. When she realized I wasn't paying attention to what she was saying, she rummaged in some inside pocket, took out a coin, and gave it to me. This gesture troubled me: she knew my passion for old coins. I felt the coin. It was a *bâttène,* a fifty-centime piece, a rare coin that circulated for a short time in Egypt around 1852. The coin I had in my hand was well worn. With my fingers I tried to reconstruct the effigies engraved on each side of it. The date of minting, 1851, was in Indian numerals. I have never understood why the Arabs gave up their own numerals, leaving them to the entire world, in order to adopt those Indian hieroglyphics in which the "2" is an inverted "6," the "8" an upside-down "7," the "5" a "0," and the "0" a mere period! On the front was a man's face with a delicate mustache, long hair, and rather large eyes. On the obverse was the same design, except that the man no longer had a mustache and had a female appearance. I later learned that the coin had been struck by the father of twins, a boy and a girl, for whom he felt a fierce passion. He was a powerful man, a feudal landowner and a political leader. This coin was not official currency; he had minted it for his own pleasure, and it circulated only on his own estates.

In 1929, in Buenos Aires, we had a twenty-centime piece known as the *zahir.* You are well aware of what this word means—the apparent, the visible. It is the opposite of the *bâttène,* which means the inner, that which is buried in the belly.

I took a magnifying glass and began to look for some particular sign that might be engraved on one of the sides of the coin. There was a cross, but that had probably occurred by chance in the course of time.

The lady observed me in silence. I invited her to sit down in an old leather armchair. She formed a small, compact figure as she sat there. When her eyes were not watching my hands feeling the coin, they roamed around the book-lined room. She seemed to be counting the books, and I noticed that her head followed the movement of her eyes. At one point she got up and went slowly to the bookcase at the back, to take out a handwritten Koran that one of King Farouk's Coptic ministers had given me on the occasion of a visit to the university of Al Azhar in Cairo.

There was something fragile, at once clumsy and graceful, in her step. She turned toward me and said, in rather bad Spanish, "What are you doing with a manuscript in Arabic?" I replied that I liked Arabic script and calligraphy and Persian miniatures. I even told her that at least once a year I went to Córdoba, to wallow in nostalgia for an earlier, happier Andalusia. I told her, too, that all the translations of the Koran that I had read had given me a powerful intuition that the Arabic text must be sublime. She nodded agreement and quietly began to read a few verses. It was a sort of murmur, something between chant and lament. I left her there, plunged in the book with the beatitude and passion of someone who had found what he had been looking for for a long time. I thought of playing for her a recording of Sheikh Abdesamad chanting the ninth Sura, "Repentance," but changed my mind. What an odd situation! I felt as if I were in a book, one of those picturesque characters who appear in the middle of a story to throw the reader off the scent; perhaps I was one book among the thousands pressed together in that library where I had long ago come to work. Besides, a book—at least that's how I see it—is a labyrinth created on purpose to confuse men, with the intention of ruining them and bringing them back to the narrow limits of their ambitions.

Thus I found myself, on that afternoon in June 1951, shut up in my library with a mysterious lady, holding between my fingers an old coin that had never even been used. At sundown the sky became infused with a mauve tinged with yellow and white. I had the sense that this was the face of a happy death. I was not afraid. I already knew that death, or the allusion to it, turns men into objects of value and pathos. I had been acquainted with it in books and dreams. I shut my eyes and there I saw, as in a flash, the face of a tormented man; in my mind he could only be the father of the lady sitting in my room reading the Koran. . . .

After that vision, I felt trapped. Not an entirely unpleasant feeling, but I would have preferred to act and not be acted upon. My imagination had to follow without intervening. I told myself that by inventing stories with living people and throwing them into forked paths or houses filled with sand, I had ended up imprisoned in this room with a character or, rather, a riddle, two faces of the same being completely entrammeled in an unfinished story, a story of ambiguity and flight!

I sat there, staking my life on heads or tails with the *bâttène*. An inner voice was telling me, with just the touch of irony required, "The morning sun gleamed on the bronze sword, on which there was no longer any trace of blood. Will you believe him? The old man hardly defended himself." I was that old man, a prisoner in a character that I could have shaped if I had stayed a little longer in Morocco or Egypt. So I had to listen to her.

The lady shut the Koran and placed it on the table between us. Having the Holy Book between us like this would make lying impossible, even though she had put it there by pure chance. The lady held out her hand to take back the coin. She examined it, placed it on the Koran, then, in a neutral tone, said: "At the point and place I've come to, I pause for a moment, take off my finery, remove all my skins one by one; like an onion I'll peel myself away before you until I come to the ultimate substance—sin, error, and shame."

After a long silence, staring at the Koran, she went on: "If I've decided to speak today, it is because I've found you at last. You alone are capable of understanding. I am not one of your characters, though I could have been. But it's not as an outline filled with sands and words that I present myself to you. For some years now, I have been a wanderer. A fugitive. I even think I'm wanted in my own country for murder, usurpation of identity, abuse of confidence, and theft of inheritance. What I'm looking for is not the truth—I'm incapable of recognizing it. Nor is it justice, for justice is impossible. In this book are verses with the force of law but that don't encompass the woman's point of view. What I'm looking for is not forgiveness; those who might have given it to me are not alive. And yet I need justice, truth, and forgiveness. I've gone from country to country with a secret desire to die forgotten and to be reborn in the shroud of a destiny washed of all suspicion. I've learned to detach my life from places and objects that crumble away as soon as they are touched. I went away, expelled from my past by myself, believing that by moving away from my native country I would find forgetfulness and peace and that I would at last earn consolation. I have left everything: the old house, the authority that I was condemned to exercise over my family, my books, the lie at the heart of my life, and the endless solitude that was imposed upon me. I could no longer simulate a life that made me ashamed."

I admit that up till now I had not understood what she was getting at. I listened to her patiently and with curiosity; she knew how to stir within me attention that kept me riveted to my chair, forgetting time. Before she came, I had felt at loose ends. I was already old, and some of my friends were dead. My sight was gradually fading—irremediably, the doctor had warned me. I prepared myself for solitude and dependency. Her visit, announced by several letters, interested me all the more in that she claimed to have been recommended to me by Stephen Albert, an old friend—long since dead. I found the ruse amusing. She did not know that Stephen was dead, or even who he really was. I had already received letters signed with the name of one of my characters. After all, I invented nothing. I read books and encyclopedias, rummaged in dictionaries, and came back with stories credible enough to please and to soothe the fear of time that each day digs our common grave a little deeper. All my life I had contrasted the power of words with the strength of the real and imaginary, visible and hidden world. I must admit, it gave me more pleasure to venture into the dream and the invisible than into what seemed to me to be violent, physical, and limited.

After a long silence, in which the lady seemed to be expecting a reply or some encouraging reaction, I said, as if in jest, something terrible, one of the few sentences I remember, because I wrote it in 1941: "He who throws himself into some atrocious act must imagine that he has already committed it, must impose upon himself a future as irrevocable as the past." I didn't realize that these words were to hurt her, but I was condemning her to continuing the way she was. By what right had I passed this sentence? I, in my retirement, not far from death, already on the verge of blindness, surrounded by layers of darkness that were slowly advancing to deprive me forever of the day, its light and its sun—why did I take such pleasure in playing with that lady's destiny?

I had to say something: I couldn't just sit there silent or indifferent. It's strange, but that woman on the verge of ruin awakened in me a memory of desire, and sometimes the memory of a more violent emotion, one stronger than reality itself. How can I explain it? For me there was more ambiguity in her presence in my room than in the story of her life. I suspected that she had not yet removed all her masks, that she was still capable of playing on both banks of the river.

Yes, this desire took me back—thirty years. I reconstructed in my mind the stages of desire that I once felt for a woman who came to borrow some books from my library. She was tall, very thin, and graceful. She spoke little and read much. I tried, through the books she borrowed, to guess her character, her secret thoughts and passions. I remember she had read all the available translations of *The Thousand and One Nights*. She read Shakespeare in the original. I thought she was training for some artistic career. I knew nothing about her.

One day we were alone in a narrow passageway between two shelves. We were back to back, each looking for a book. She turned around toward me and by a strange and happy coincidence our hands fell almost simultaneously on the same book: *Don Quixote*. I was secretly getting it for her, not to introduce her to something new, but to suggest she reread it. Our two bodies were so close to each other that I felt rise up inside me a wave of warmth of a kind that shy people know only too well. Her hair brushed across my face.

She went off with the book, and I never saw her again. Sometimes I think about her and relive that disturbing moment. There are emotions that mark you for life, and ever since, without admitting it, I have looked for that face, that body, that furtive appearance. Now I have lost all hope of ever finding her again, and even if I did, I would be very unhappy.

The image of this woman visits me from time to time in a dream that always turns into a nightmare. She walks slowly toward me, her hair windswept. She smiles, then runs off. Running after her, I find myself in a large Andalusian house with intercommunicating rooms. Then, just before leaving the house, and this is where the unpleasant part begins, she stops and allows me to approach. I have almost caught her when I realize that she is a man dressed as a woman, a drunken soldier. I leave the labyrinth of the house and find myself in a valley, then in a swamp, then on a plain surrounded by mirrors to infinity.

Since I lost sight of her, I have had nothing but nightmares. I am haunted by my own books.

When you're blind you live on nostalgia, which for me is a luminous mist, the background of my past. Night falls constantly over my eyes; it is a long twilight. If I praise shadow, it is because this long night has given me back a desire to rediscover and to touch things. I travel constantly. I retrace my steps in my dream-nightmares. I travel to verify not the landscapes but the scents, the sounds, the smells of a town or country. I find any excuse to travel abroad. I have never traveled so much as since I went blind! I still think that everything is given to the writer for him to use: pain as well as pleasure, oblivion as well as memory. Perhaps, in the end, I shall know who I am. But that's another story.

As this old man was speaking, his hands placed one on top of the other on his stick, he was gradually surrounded by people of all sorts. The café was becoming a kind of classroom, and he like a university professor giving a lecture to his students. People were fascinated by that sightless face—attracted, too, by his slightly husky voice. They listened to this visitor from another century, from a distant, almost unknown country.

He had sensed, from the noise of the chairs and then the silence that reigned in the café, that he had an attentive audience. At one point he stopped and asked: "Are you there? I came to this country, driven by my solitude, and I am seeking you in the depths of the night, a princess who has escaped from a fairy tale. You who are listening to me, if you see her, tell her that *the man who was beloved of the moon* is there, that I am the secret and the slave, love and night."

The audience remained silent. Suddenly a man got up and said, "You are welcome here. Tell us about this woman who gave you the coin. What did she tell you?"

Another voice rose from the back of the café: "Yes! What did this woman tell you?"

The blind man made a gesture for the audience to be patient, took a sip of tea, then resumed his story:

The woman was fearful; she tried not to show it, but one can sense such things. She must have been afraid, as if pursued by vengeance, bad conscience, or simply by the police. I don't know if she really had committed the crime of which she accused herself. I know that she had followed a stranger, an Arab from South America, an Egyptian or a Lebanese merchant who had come to buy carpets and jewelry. She left with him, believing that this would help her escape her past. For the man it was a love story, for her a way out. And yet she lived with this rich merchant for some years. She did not give him a child. The man was unhappy. Her life was a burden, and she often said, "I shall live to forget myself," those same words. The man was a merchant, not a poet. He was overcome by her beauty and fragility. At first she wanted to help him in his business, but that annoyed him. She spent whole days in a big house situated in the northern quarter of Buenos Aires. She didn't tell me this, but I later learned from Fernando Torres, the author of *Unfinished Report,* that strange things had taken place in the Arab merchant's house.

On her first visit, she spoke little. The second time— it was seventeen days later—she spoke a little more, but revealed no secrets. She seemed to me to be someone on the run, wounded, on the edge of a cliff. She spoke of disappearing, of merging into the sand. She said that she was pursued night and day by the people she had injured. When she stopped complaining, she added with a sigh, "After all, I don't even know who I am!" What I remember of her confession is that she was guilty of at least three

146

crimes: living someone else's life, leaving someone to die, and lying. This did not seem criminal to me, it seemed more like a riddle. I was fascinated by this woman. Long after her departure, I felt an urgent wish to look for her, speak to her, question her about her life. She cultivated mystery. She was perhaps the only one not to talk about labyrinths, mirrors, and tigers. In any case, she was the last face that my sight was to register for eternity.

At the time I was just fifty-five. A whole part of my life had come to an end, for blindness is a closure; but it is also a liberation, a solitude favorable to inventions, a key, and an algebra. I decided to change, not my perception, but my preoccupations. My life had been devoted mainly to books. I had written them, published them, destroyed them, read them, loved them—I had spent all my life in books. This woman, sent by a beneficent hand, came just before my night fell to give me a last image, to offer my memory her face, entirely turned toward a past that I could only guess at. I told myself that this was no accident, that it must be the work of some beneficent, anonymous power: I was to carry into my subterranean journey an image of living beauty. I can say today that I have worked hard on that face, whose lines have often eluded me. Was it the image of an image, a mere illusion, a veil placed over a life, or a metaphor elaborated in a dream? I know that my interest in that face, in that intrusion into my exhausted privacy, gave me back my youth, the courage to travel and to go in search of something, or someone.

Before setting out on the trail of that face, I had to rid myself of a few secrets. I no longer had to keep them. I went to a place where the stream of the Maldonado—it is now buried—passed, and washed myself with the smooth stone, that very stone that replaces water for the ablutions of Muslims in the desert. I performed my ablutions, thinking of the friends who had gone and of everything that they had entrusted me with before their death. Only that Arab woman's secret remained there, in my rib cage. This alone protected me, and I knew nothing about it, except the story of a disguise that turned out badly. The coin was a sign to guide me in my search.

It was while walking recently through the gardens of Alhambra, drowned in the perfumes of fresh soil that had just been dug by the Spanish gardeners for planting roses, that I had a very strong intuition that this face was a soul burdened with torments, and that the journey would have to continue as far as Tétouan, Fez, and Marrakesh.

There is something of a pilgrimage about this journey. I must carry it out without interruption until I have returned that soul to the peace, serenity, and silence that it needs. It is a soul in chains. That woman may have been dead for a long time, but I still hear her voice: it doesn't speak, just whispers or moans. I am accustomed to that pain, and only the soil of this country, its light, its smells, will return it to peace. She would have liked to tell me her story without mitigating the parts of it that she found unbearable, but she preferred to leave me signs to decipher.

The first metaphor is a ring containing seven keys to open the seven gates of the city. Each gate that opens will give peace to her soul. It was while reading the *Novel of Al Mo'atasim,* an anonymous manuscript found in the fifteenth century beneath a flagstone of the mosque in Córdoba, that I realized the meaning of this first gift. A storyteller from the far South tried to penetrate these gates, but destiny or malevolence prevented the poor man from succeeding.

The second object she gave me was a small clock without hands, made in 1851, the exact year when that fifty-centime coin was minted in Egypt. She also gave me a prayer mat on which is reproduced, in a disordered pattern, the famous *Wedding Night of Shozroez and Hirin,* a Persian miniature illustrating a manuscript of the Khamseh, the work of the poet Nizamy. This meant insolence. No good Muslim would ever say his prayers on an erotic design from the seventeenth century! I have tried to decipher the secret order relating the seven keys, the clock, and the coin. I don't believe I have found it. However, the last thing she gave me was not an object but an account of a dream that begins with a poem she attributed to Firdusi, who lived in the tenth century. I shall read you the poem, as she wrote it out:

> *In that closed body, he is a girl*
> *whose face is more brilliant than the sun.*
> *From top to toe she is like ivory,*
> *her cheeks like the sky, her waist like a willow.*
> *On her silver shoulders are two dark braids of hair,*
> *whose ends are like the rings of a chain.*
> *In that closed body, he is an old, worn face,*
> *a wound, a shadow, and a tumult,*
> *a body concealed in another body. . . .*

As you may have realized, the poem has been altered. That is the extent of her distress. The dream leads us to the gates of the desert, in that Orient imagined by the writers and painters.

149

18

The Andalusian Night

The dream was precise and very dense. I set out in search
of a long, dark braid of hair. I went out into the streets of
Buenos Aires, guided, like a sleepwalker, by the delicate
scent of a fine head of hair. Catching a glimpse of it in the
crowd, I hastened on; it disappeared. And so I continued
my pursuit until I found myself outside the city, lost in
piles of stone and burned calves' heads, surrounded by
those unknown quarters that we now call shantytowns,
alone, oppressed by the smell of burning flesh and stared
at by a gang of half-naked kids brandishing pieces of wood
shaped into rifles, playing at being guerrillas. When I tried
to run away, my legs refused to move. I felt I might suffocate.

Just then I caught a glimpse of the black hair once more.
I was saved. I left the shantytown without difficulty. A
few hundred yards farther on, a half-glimpsed figure gestured to me to follow her. I obeyed and found myself in
the middle of the medina of an Arab town. No dark head

of hair was to be seen. There was no one to lead me on. I was alone, but relieved and even happy to walk through those narrow, shady alleyways.

Not all the women were veiled. With good humor the men were praising their merchandise. They were selling spices of every color, Turkish slippers, carpets, woolen blankets, dried fruit. Some shouted, others sang. The medina appeared to my eyes as a tangle of places—streets and squares—in which every kind of miracle was possible. Thrown from an Argentinian shantytown into an Arab medina, I walked in a daze, in which everything astonished me. The streets were crammed with vendors and old beggars. A knife grinder who had his grindstone mounted on a bicycle announced his presence by whistling into a sort of plastic harmonica, which gave out a strident sound, recognizable from afar. There was the water seller, an old, bent man who uttered a long, painful cry—something between a threatening wolf and an abandoned dog—to praise the freshness and benefits of the spring water contained in the black skin slung across his back. There were also beggars, endlessly repeating the same, mechanical litany, hands outstretched, motionless, eternal. The street would not have existed without them; it belonged to them.

I don't know how, but suddenly I knew that the water seller, the knife grinder, and one of the beggars, a blind man, were part of the story that I was living through. I saw them as partners. I was also convinced that they were in league, to trace the path that I would take and to compose, by their cries and attitudes, the same face and frail, unsteady body swept this way and that by a story woven by alleyways. I watched the three men posted in the medina like shadows moving with the sun.

I was in pain, but couldn't say where. Concentrating on that pain, crouching at the entrance to a mosque, I saw, like an apparition, the face of a young woman, puffy, distorted by some inner pain. I saw the face, then the tiny body crouching in a large shopping basket—the legs must have been folded or rooted in the ground. I was the only one to see this brutal image in the alleyway, which was probably on the other side of the mosque. Suddenly everything went dark. The medina became a city of darkness, and I heard only the funereal litany of the three men. Their shrill, nasal voices described the features of the face I had seen. It was more than a vision, it was a presence; I could feel its breath and warmth.

This dream pursued me for several days. I no longer dared leave my library, fearful of night and sleep. The black hair was the extended hand of death, pushing me toward nothingness. In order to rid myself of this obsession, I decided to undertake the journey described in the dream. After all, between death and me there could not have been more than a season left. I might as well anticipate the ordeal. I forgot to tell you that in the medina the currency in circulation was none other than the fifty-centime coin, the *bâttène,* though there were also bank notes dating from our own time.

Friends! You have listened to the stranger with patience and hospitality. But since this story and its characters have roamed my night, my soul has grown weary. I thought death would come suddenly, without warning, without ceremony. I was wrong. It has taken a winding path—which I do not find unpleasant! It has taken its time. My soul awoke and my body rose up and began to walk. I followed it without asking questions. I crossed Europe. I stopped in Andalusia.

Despite my age and my latest infirmity, I indulged myself: I spent a whole day in the palace of the Alhambra. I sensed things. I smelled soil and stone. I stroked the walls and let my hand trail over the marble. So I was visiting the Alhambra for the first time with my eyes extinguished. At the end of the day, I hid myself in the Moorish bath. The guards saw nothing, so I shut myself up in the palace and garden. Night fell at about nine o'clock. It was July, a mild night. I emerged from my hiding place like a child. What bliss! I trembled with pleasure. I walked without groping; listened to the murmur of the water; breathed in deeply the scent of jasmine, roses, and lemon trees; listened to the echo of Andalusian music, played here five centuries before. When the orchestra stopped playing, the muezzin called to prayer in his harsh, strong voice. I thought of the kings, princes, philosophers, scientists leaving this kingdom, abandoning the country and its secrets to the cross of the infidel. With my hands on the marble, it was farewell to the day, the end of nostalgia, farewell to that old memory. I spent a night of disturbing euphoria. Beloved of the moon, I merged my night in the mildness of the night that covered Alhambra. I thought I had rediscovered my sight for a brief moment in that Andalusian night, a night illuminating my night, an outraged solitude, displaced in time, left behind the wall.

There were voices. Festivities. Poets recited verses that I knew by heart, and I spoke them along with the poets. I walked, following the voices. I arrived at the Courtyard of the Lions; the heavy silence of an immobile time reigned there. I sat on the ground as if someone had ordered me to halt.

I could no longer hear the poets.

I sought my voice in the memory of myself. The first memory was of the youth that I was, accompanying his father, who was already blind, through these same gardens. Suddenly a woman's voice, deep and mocking, reached me from outside. I was expecting it. She slowly articulated the first letters of the Arabic alphabet: *alif* . . . *ba* . . . *ta* . . . *jim* . . . *ha* . . . *dal* . . . The chanted letters echoed around the courtyard.

I stayed there until dawn without moving, my ears attentive, my hands gripping the marble. It was a woman's voice in a man's body. Just before the first glimmers of daylight, two strong hands seized my neck, trying to strangle me. I fought back with the last strength remaining to me—such strength is the most terrible; I had a physical power I had not suspected. With my stick I lashed out. Without letting go, the man uttered a cry of pain. I felt his body shift slightly to the left. With that same strength, I got up and delivered a mighty blow to the strangler.

Was it a human being, an angel of misfortune, a ghost, a bird condemned to die alone? Was it a man or a woman? Did I really live through that hand-to-hand fight with a veiled man, or did I dream this incident in the dream of the Andalusian night? I know that by morning I was exhausted and my neck ached.

The young man who accompanied me must have been worried. He realized that I had got myself locked in, for he was waiting for me early in the morning at the main entrance. I was happy, despite tiredness and lack of sleep. I now know that the body that had thrown itself upon me

154

during the night wore a thick, long wig. It must have been death. The death that still mocks me came close to me, then moved away with the same evil delight, the same insolence. That night was probably supposed to be my last. I would have had a fine death in that night at Granada, but I fought back with all the fury of a young man. I felt free, delivered of that slow, painful wait. Now it can come. I know its face. I know its voice. I know its hands. I know many things about it, but, like everybody else, I know neither the hour nor the day of its coming. For some years now I have gone on walking. I walk slowly, like someone who has come from so far that he no longer expects to arrive. . . .

Where am I now? I smell the strong scent of fresh mint, I hear the voice of fruit sellers, I detect the aroma of cooking. We must be near some small, cheap restaurant. . . . Strong smells, mixed with burning kerosene—all this is intoxicating for an old man who has walked for such a long time. Am I the object of some conspiracy? Tell me now, you who hold my fate in your hands, would they have found a corpse or a book in one of the palaces of Córdoba, Toledo, or Granada?

Did I dream the Andalusian night, or did I live through it? Your silence is harsh. But I am familiar with the land of your ancestors, and close to that twilight that is coming upon you and enveloping you. All this was done by a woman who conceived the excessive, the impossible, the unthinkable. . . .

I, too, could quote from the diwan of Almoqtadir El Maghrebi, who lived in the twelfth century, and, without identifying myself with the reciter, I will recall this *cuarteta*:

Murieron otros, pero ello aconteció en el pasado,
Que es la estación (nadie lo ignora) mas propicia a la
   muerte,
¿Es posible que yo, súbdito de Yaqub Almansur,
Muera como tuvieron que morir las rosas y Aristóteles?

Others died, but this happened in the past,
Which is the season (as everyone knows) most favorable
   to death.
Is it possible that I, a subject of Yaqub Almansur,
Must, like Aristotle and roses, die in turn?

19

The Gate of the Sands

A man with small gray eyes, almost closed with exhaustion and time, a beard reddened with henna, his head wrapped in a blue turban, was stretched out on the ground like a wounded animal. He looked toward the stranger, who had just sunk into a deep sleep. The stranger's eyes were open but raised to the ceiling, unseeing, letting pass dreams, mirrors, fountains, butterflies, and the day.

The men and women didn't move. They were afraid to awaken the stranger too suddenly, for he was the prisoner of a secret that intrigued them. Thinking about what he had said, they waited. The light of the fading day gave shadows to the simplest objects, animated them with colors and a brief glory, passed over faces, caught a look for an instant, then swept away without disturbing anything. The man with gray eyes tried to rise. Having trouble regaining the use of his legs, he leaned on a stool and slowly dragged himself to the café door. He was entirely enveloped in his worn, dirty burnous. One could hardly see his face, which he hid with part of his turban. Under his arm he carried an old briefcase.

He came up to the waiting, motionless throng, stopped, and sat on a squeaky chair; a man gestured to him not to make any noise, but the broken old chair squeaked. He asked for a glass of water. A neighbor offered him his, which was half full. The old man took out of his briefcase a pinch of yellow powder, dissolved it in the water, and swallowed it, murmuring an appeal to God to shorten his pains and cure him. Then he put down the glass, gave a nod of thanks to his neighbor, placed his briefcase on the table, opened it, and took out a large, well-thumbed notebook. Without warning, he raised the book in the air and declared, "Everything is here . . . as God is my witness. . . ."

The people shifted their attention from the sleeping stranger, abandoning him to his sleep. "Everything is here . . . and you know it," repeated the man in the blue turban. These words, said over and over several times by a familiar voice, functioned like a magic key that opens forgotten or condemned doors. Pointing to the blind man, he said: "We will be the poorer when that man is dead. An infinite number of things—stories, dreams, and countries—will die with him. That is why I am here. I am with you once more for a few hours, for a few days. Things have changed since I was here last. Some of you have gone away, others have come. Between us there are ashes and forgetfulness. Between you and me lies a long absence, a desert where I wandered, a mosque where I lived, a terrace where I read and wrote, a grave in which I slept. It has taken me some time to reach this city, where I recognize neither places nor men. I left, driven from the great square. I walked for a long time through plains and centuries.

Everything is here . . . as God is my witness."

He paused for a moment, stared at the big notebook, opened it, turned the pages: they were empty. If you examined them closely, you could see that there were still traces of ink, bits of sentences in pale ink, small, simple pencil drawings. He went on: "The book is empty. Ruined. I was imprudent enough to leaf through it one night. As the beams from the full moon fell on it, the light effaced the words, one after another. Nothing remains of what time consigned to this book. . . . Of course there are a few snatches here and there, a few syllables, but the moon has taken our story away from us. What can a storyteller do when the moon robs him so shamelessly? Condemned to silence, to flight, and to wandering, I wanted to forget. I did not succeed. I met charlatans and bandits, wandered with nomadic tribes who invaded towns. I have known droughts, times when all the cattle have died, the despair of the men of the plains. I have scoured the country from north to south and from south to infinity."

The blind man woke. His head moved. His open eyes rested on nothingness. He got up. An empty chair fell over, making an unpleasant noise. A boy rushed up and held him by the arm, and together they went off to the great square, which was quiet at that hour. The old man whispered a few words in the boy's ear; the boy stopped for a moment, then walked over to a circle of men and women sitting on mats on the floor of the café, around a lady who was dressed entirely in white and who was talking slowly. Room was made for the blind man, who sat down, crosslegged. All his attention was concentrated on the woman's voice. Thus he passed from a story to which he believed he held the keys, to a tale of which he knew neither the beginning nor the meaning. He was happy to find himself embarked in the middle of a sentence, as if his journey in the medina were following a course dictated by his wishes, as if he were trying desperately to lose his way and to sink into the labyrinth that he had designed for himself in his Buenos Aires library. The woman did not stop: ". . . to the touch, as for seeing! But, then, this sword was merely the vision of a prince possessed! Yet the blade shone in the midday sun, and the men were washing the paving stones where the blood had clotted. . . ."

The blind man nodded agreement.

On the other side of the square, in the café, the man in the blue turban continued his story:

If our city has seven gates, it is because it was beloved of seven saints. But this love has become a curse, as I have known ever since I dared to recount the story and destiny of the eighth birth. Death is there, outside, turning like fortune's wheel. It has a face, hands, and a voice. I know it. It has accompanied my steps for a long time. I have become familiar with its cynicism; it no longer frightens me. It has taken away all the characters in my tales.

I left in the evening, in the middle of the story, promising to tell my faithful audience the following day the rest of the adventures. When I came back, the story was already over. During the night, death had seized the main characters. So I found myself with scraps of the story, scraps unable to live and breathe. My imagination was ruined. I tried to justify the sudden disappearances. My audience would not go along with me. Death, whose mocking laughter I could hear in the distance, was turning me into a clown. I rambled on, stammering. I was no longer a storyteller but a charlatan, a puppet manipulated by the fingers of death.

At first I didn't understand what was happening. I blamed my memory, my old-man's memory. It wasn't even that I had dried up—I still had a good stock of stories. But the instant I began to tell them, they were emptied of their substance. I spent sleepless nights. It was during one of these nights that death appeared to me in the form of a character, the eighth birth, Ahmed or Zahra, and threatened me with all heaven's thunderbolts. He reproached me for betraying the secret, for soiling by my presence the empire of the secret, the place where Es-ser El Mekhfi, the supreme secret, is kept hidden deep in the earth. I saw madness approaching. I no longer had a face that I could show the public, and I was ashamed. The curse had fallen upon me. Neither you nor I would ever know the end of the story, which could not pass through all the gates. I had to hide myself.

I tried other things, other occupations. A public writer—I had no customers. A quack—I had no success. I played the lute—people blocked up their ears. Nothing worked. I was cursed, cursed and hopeless.

I made a pilgrimage to the far south of the country. I arrived after months of walking and wandering through strange villages, which, in my madness, must have been only apparitions, empty bodies, set down on my way by death, which was mocking me. I remember one evening when I was tired I fell asleep under a tree in a desert place where there was nothing but stones and a tree. When I woke the next morning, I found myself in a cemetery where people dressed in white were burying a number of youths in a big ditch, without shrouds, naked. I was horrified. When I went up to the ditch, I thought I recognized my son. I yelled out. A strong hand was placed over my mouth to stifle my cry. I went away, as if guided by in-

161

stinct. I walked for a long time, then found myself back at my starting point. The characters I thought I had invented appeared on my way, called to me, and demanded an explanation. Condemning fingers pointed at me, accusing me of betrayal.

Ahmed's father locked me up in an old building and forced me to go back to the square and tell the story a different way. He was an embittered, brutal man, probably on the threshold of hell. The mother was behind him, in a small wheelchair. She kept spitting on the ground. Her lackluster eyes were fixed on me; they terrified me. I met Fatima, too. She was no longer sick. It was on a Friday. She stopped me and said, "I am Fatima; I am cured." She appeared to me laden with flowers, happy, like someone who had just taken her revenge on destiny. A slight smile played around her lips. Her white dress—something between a shroud and a wedding dress—was almost intact; just a little soil was caught in the folds. "Do you recognize me now?" she asked calmly. "I am the woman you chose to be your hero's victim. You soon got rid of me. I have now come back to visit the places and observe the things that I wanted to be eternal. I see that the country hasn't changed. And you are lost—you have lost your story and your reason. The land is dry, especially in the South. I didn't know the South. I am following in the footsteps of your story. I count the dead and await the survivors. You can do nothing to me. I belong to that eternity of which you speak without knowledge. The country hasn't changed—things have even got worse.

"Strange! People spend their lives being abused; every day they are humiliated, and they don't react; then one day they go out into the streets and smash everything. The army intervenes and fires on the crowd to re-establish order. Silence. They dig a big ditch and throw the bodies in. It's becoming chronic. When I was sick, I didn't see what was happening around me. I was struggling with my fits and awaiting deliverance. Now I hear everything, especially the cries of the children and the gunshots. It's stupid to die of a stray bullet when one isn't even twenty, and confused. Poor children! . . ."

She paused for a moment, took out some dates from a pocket hidden by the flowers, and offered me some: "Here, eat these dates, they're good. Don't be afraid—these aren't the ones they put on a dead man's face in place of eyes. No, I picked them myself this morning. Eat them—you'll see more clearly! . . ."

Indeed, upon eating them, I saw clearly. Dazzled by a strong light, I saw shadows carved out of a white brightness. Of course, nobody was near me now. Fatima had disappeared. I rubbed my eyes till they hurt. I was completely possessed by this story and its people.

A story is like a house, an old house, with different levels, rooms, corridors, doors, and windows. Locks, cellars, useless spaces. The walls are its memory. Scratch the stone a little, hold your ear to it, and you will hear things! Time gathers together what the day brings and what night disperses. It keeps and holds. Stone is the witness. Each stone is a page of writing, read and crossed out. A story. A house. A book. A desert. A journey. Repentance and forgiveness. Did you know that to forgive is to hide? I have no glory or splendor to carry me to heaven. I have forgotten the five prayers. I believed that the spring from which I drew my stories would never dry up, like the ocean, like clouds moving across the sky, changing but always giving rain.

I seek forgiveness. Who would dare give me that oblivion? Someone told me that an anonymous poet who became a saint of the sands, which cover up and hide, might help me. I set off in search of him. I divested myself of everything and followed the caravan on foot. I wore nothing but woolen clothes and took the road to the South without looking back. I no longer had any family, any occupation, any ties. Before, I lived without caring about tomorrow. I had my own circle in the great square, a faithful and attentive audience. My stories gave me enough to live on. I slept in peace. I rummaged around in ancient manuscripts. I stole stories from others, until the day when a poor woman from Alexandria came to see me. She was slim and dark: her eyes saw things in their true light. Of all the storytellers on the square, whose stories she had followed, she chose me. She said: "I have listened to all of you, and only you would be capable of telling the story of my uncle who was in fact my aunt. I need to be delivered of the weight of this riddle, a secret that has long weighed on our family. My uncle's true identity was discovered on the day of his death. Ever since, we have lived through a nightmare. I thought that making this story public might turn it into a legend; as everybody knows, myths and legends are more bearable than harsh reality."

She recounted in detail the story of Bey Ahmed. It took two days. I listened to her, thinking the whole time what I could do with this material, and how it could be adapted to our country. After all, there is very little difference between our two societies: they are both Arabic and Muslim, feudal and traditional. I asked her why she chose me. She said, perhaps to flatter me, that I had more imagination than the rest. Then she added: "Now the story is in you. It will occupy your days and nights, dig its bed in your body and your mind. You will not be able to escape it. It's a story that comes from far away. It is acquainted with death. Now that I have told it, I feel better—lighter, younger. I leave you a treasure and a deep well. Be careful—you must not confuse them. The same goes for your reason. Be worthy of the secret and its wounds. Pass on the story through the seven gardens of the soul. Farewell, my friend, my accomplice!"

Before leaving me, she handed me a large notebook of over two hundred pages; it contained the journal and thoughts of Bey Ahmed. I read it, reread it. Each time I was overcome, at a loss to know what I could do with this story. Then I began to tell it. The farther I got, the more I sank into the well; my characters began to desert me. . . . Eventually I had to admit failure. Taking advantage of the clearing of the square, I headed off along the road to the South.

When the book was emptied of its writing by the full moon, I was afraid at first. But these were the first signs of my deliverance. In the end I, too, forgot everything. If any of you really wants to know how this story ended, he will have to ask the moon when it is full. I now lay down before you the book, the inkwell, and the pens. I shall now go away and read the Koran on the tomb of the dead!